THE HOUSEHOLD OF
SIR THOMAS MORE

THE HOUSEHOLD OF SIR THOMAS MORE

ANNE MANNING,
REV. W. H. HUTTON

ISBN: 978-93-5344-908-7

Published: 1899

· LIBELLVS · A · MARGARETA · MORE · ·
· QVINDECIM · ANNOS · NATA ·
· CHELSELÆ · INCEPTVS ·

Nvlla dies sive linea

MOTTO OF MARGARET MORE.
Designed by Herbert Railton

**LIBELLUS A MARGARETA MORE QVINDECIM
ANNOS NATA CHELSELÆ INCEPTVS**
Nvlla dies sine linea

"ANON WE SIT DOWN TO REST AND TALK."
Drawn by John Jellicoe and Herbert Railton

THE HOUSEHOLD OF
SIR THOMAS MORE

WITH AN INTRODUCTION BY
THE REV. W. H. HUTTON, B.D.

FELLOW OF S. JOHN'S COLLEGE, OXFORD

AND TWENTY-FIVE ILLUSTRATIONS
BY JOHN JELLICOE AND HERBERT RAILTON

MDCCCXCIX

LIST OF ILLUSTRATIONS

Page

INTRODUCTION

It is not always from the closest and most accurate historian that we receive the truest picture of an age or of a character. The artist gives a more real picture than the photographer; and it needs imagination and sympathy, as well as labour and research, to make a hero of old time live again to-day. The minutest investigation will hardly better the vivid reality of Scott's James I. or Charles II., or portray more truly than Mr. Shorthouse has done the fragile yet fascinating personality of Charles I. Yet to say this is not to undervalue history or to contemn the labour of true students. Rather, without their aid we cannot rightly see the past at all: it comes to us only with the distortions of our own prejudice and our narrow modern outlook. We need both the work of the scholar and the imagination of the artist. Without the first we could not behold the past, without the second we could not understand it.

In religion, in politics, in art, in all that makes life beautiful and men true, we must know the past if we would use the present or provide for the future. And our knowledge is barren indeed if it does not touch the intimacies of human existence. What we must know is how men lived and thought, not merely how they acted. We must see them in the home, and not only in the senate or the field. It is thus that the Letters of Erasmus, or Luther's Table Talk, are worth a ton of Sleidan's dreary commentaries or Calvin's systematic theology. And yet we cannot dispense with either. We must study past ages as a whole, and then bring the imagination of the artist and the poet to show us the truth and the passion that lies nearest to their heart. It is thus, then, in history that the imaginary portrait has its valued place.

Saturated with contemporary literature, yet alive to the influences of a wider life, the student who is also an artist turns to a great movement, and with the touch of genius fixes the true impression of its soul in poetry, on canvas, or in prose. Such was the work of Walter Pater. He taught us, through the delicate study of a secondary but most alluring painter, to "understand to how great a place in human culture the art of Italy had been called." In his picture of a great scholar and a beautiful, pathetic, childlike soul, he showed the fascination of that priceless truth—that what men have thought and done, that what has interested and charmed them, can never wholly die—"no language they have spoken, nor oracle beside which they have hushed their voices, no dream which has once been entertained by actual human minds, nothing about which they have ever been passionate or expended time and zeal."

And more. He taught us not only how to understand the past, but he showed us how it understood itself. "A Prince of Court Painters"—Watteau, as he was seen by one who loved him, by a sympathetic woman—like all such, the keenest of critics, yet the tenderest of hearts—is given to us as not even pictures or personal letters could give. Sebastian van Storck, Duke Carl of Rosenmold—they are portraits, though it is only imagination that makes them live.

I remember Mr. Freeman once saying to me, as he took me his favourite walk at Somerleaze, that he had read a study of Mr. Pater's—a strange mediæval story of Denys l'Auxerrois—and could not be satisfied till he knew what it meant. Was it true? It was a question befitting one who had made the past to live again. Truth was the first, almost the only, thing the historian prized. Denys the organ-builder may never have watched the decoration of the Cathedral of Saint Étienne, or made, by the mere sight of him, the old feel young again. And yet Walter Pater had painted a true portrait, as so often did Robert Browning, though it were imaginary; and the artist as well as the historian had imaged for us the reality of a past age.

Mr. Pater, though the most perfect artist of this school, was not the first. Humbler writers have long endeavoured to draw the great heroes as they thought their contemporaries saw them, by a fiction of memoir, or correspondence, or journal. And the "Prince of Court Painters" is a sketch in the same medium as "The Household of Sir Thomas More."

This charming book has passed through many editions, but its author, of her own choice, remained almost unknown. The "Dictionary of National Biography" has strangely passed her by. Almost all that her wishes suffer us to know is that she was sister of Mr. William Oke Manning, to whom she affectionately dedicated the fourth edition of the book which is now reprinted; that she was never married; and that she was a genuine student and an indefatigable writer on historical and literary subjects. In "Mary Powell" she touched the heart of her generation, and few books of its day had a wider circulation. "The Household of Sir Thomas More" is a still more painstaking study, and a more complete and delightful portrait. Its perfect sympathy and its quaint charm of manner secured for it a welcome even among those who claimed for the hero and his opinions a sanctity which Miss Manning's historical judgment did not ratify. Cardinal Manning, writing on March 11, 1887, rejoiced at its republication, and said: "The book is a singularly beautiful one, and I regret that I had not the pleasure of knowing the writer, whose mental gifts were of a very high order." Miss Manning was a keen critic of the Romanism of the Reformation period, as her Appendices to the fourth edition of her book show; but she did not suffer her own opinions to destroy her sympathy for him whom Reginald Pole called "the best of all the English."

"The Household of Sir Thomas More" is an imaginary portrait of a noble character. It professes to be the journal begun by Margaret, More's eldest daughter, most learned and best beloved, when she was but fifteen years old, and continued till she had taken her father's head from the pole whereon it was exposed, to treasure it till she should lay it on her breast as she too passed into the peace of God. Among "fair women" the heroic daughter is immortal:—

> "Morn broaden'd on the borders of the dark
> Ere I saw her, who clasped in her last trance

Her murder'd father's head."

So Tennyson recorded the pathetic legend with which Miss Manning ended her beautiful book.

When she wrote, it was not so hard as it is now to recall the London of Henry VIII. Miss Manning herself described very happily in 1859 what she remembered many years before.

"When we say," she wrote, "that some of our happiest and earliest years were spent on the site of Sir Thomas More's country house in the 'village of palaces,' some of our readers will hardly believe we can mean Chelsea. But, in those days, the gin-palace and tea-garden were not; Cremorne was a quiet, aristocratic seclusion, where old Queen Charlotte

'Would sometimes counsel take, and sometimes tea.'

"A few old, quiet streets and rows, with names and sites dear to the antiquary, ran down to the Thames, then a stranger to steamboats; a row of noble elms along its strand lent their deep shade to some quaint old houses with heavy architraves, picturesque flights of steps, and elaborate gates; while Queen Elizabeth's Walk, the Bishop's Walk, and the Bishop's Palace gave a kind of dignity to the more modern designations of the neighbourhood.

"When the Thames was the great highway, and every nobleman had his six or eight oared barge, the banks of the river as high as Chelsea were studded with country houses. At the foot of Battersea Bridge, which in those days did not disfigure the beautiful reach, Sir Thomas More, then a private gentleman and eminent lawyer in full practice, built the capital family house which was afterwards successively occupied by the Marquis of Winchester, Lord Dacre, Lord Burleigh, Sir Robert Cecil, the Earl of Lincoln, Sir Arthur Gorges, Lord Middlesex, the first Duke of Buckingham, Sir Bulstrode Whitlock, the second Duke of Buckingham, the Earl of Bristol, and the Duke of Beaufort. It stood about a hundred yards from the river; its front exhibited a projecting porch in the centre, and four bay windows alternating with eight large casements; while its back presented a confused assemblage of jutting casements, pent-houses, and gables in picturesque intricacy of detail, affording 'coigns of vantage,' we doubt not, to many a tuft of golden moss and stone-crop. This dwelling, which for convenience and beauty of situation and interior comfort was so highly prized by its many and distinguished occupants, appears at length to have been pulled down when it became rickety and untenantable from sheer old age—in Ossian's words, 'gloomy, windy, and full of ghosts.'"

Nor was Miss Manning obliged to rely only on her memory for a picture of More's house as it had been. The site, when she knew it, was like the New Place at Stratford-on-Avon, where only a few stones and foundations enable us to picture how stood the house where Shakespeare died. But while the household was still fresh in men's minds, and More was beginning to be reverenced as a martyr and a saint, Ellis Heywood published at Florence, in 1556, his sketch, "Il Moro," in which he set in a true description of the Chelsea garden an imaginary picture of the Chancellor and his friends talking on matters of high import to soul and spirit. "From one part of the garden," he tells us, "almost the whole of the noble city of

London was visible, and from another the beautiful Thames, with green meadows and wooded hills all around." The garden had its own charm too. "It was crowned with an almost perpetual verdure, and the branches of the fruit-trees that grew near were interwoven in a manner so beautiful that it seemed like a living tapestry worked by Nature herself."

So wrote Ellis Heywood of the external beauty of the scene. Of the inner harmony Erasmus had written years before to Ulrich von Hutten:—"More has built himself a house at Chelsea. There he lives with his wife, his son, his daughter-in-law, his three daughters and their husbands, with eleven grandchildren. There is not a man alive so loving as he: he loves his old wife as if she were indeed a young maiden." For Dame Alice, whom More had wedded very soon after the death of his first child-wife, was *nec bella nec puella*—neither a beauty nor a girl. And besides these, in the year when little Margaret, according to Miss Manning, began to write in her "fayr Libellus" which her tutor, Master Gunnel, gave her, there were dwelling in the house the aged father, Sir John More, good judge and humorous man, with his third wife.

"And the household," said Erasmus, "was a very 'platonic academy'—were it not," he adds, "an injustice to compare it with an academy where disputations concerning numbers and figures were only occasionally mingled with discussion on the moral virtues. I should rather call his house a school of Christianity; for though there is no one in it who does not study the liberal sciences, the special care of all is piety and virtue. No quarrelling or ill-tempered words are ever heard, and idleness is never seen."

In such a household it was that Margaret, More's dearest and most heroic child, was nurtured:—

> "As it were
> An angel-watered lily, that near God
> Grows and is quiet."

She was one of those fine souls to whom come alike learning and love, and in whom religion shows its fairest fruits. Holbein draws her with a Seneca in her hand, but not far away is her prayer-desk. All the children answered to their father's careful culture, for it is an idle tale that makes young John More but a silly fellow. Elizabeth, who married Mr. Dancey, Cecily, who became the wife of Giles Heron, a ward of her father's, the step-daughter Alice, who became Lady Alington, and the adopted child, Margaret Giggs, whom young Clement, sometime their fellow-scholar, wedded, were all instructed in humane letters. But Margaret was the flower of them all. To her her father wrote when she was still but a child:—

"I cannot tell you, dearest Margaret, how pleasant to me are your most delightful letters. Now, as I was reading them there chanced to be with me that noble youth, Reginald Pole—not so highly ennobled, indeed, by birth as by learning and every virtue. To him your letter seemed a miracle, even before he knew how you were beset by shortness of time and other hindrances. And hardly would he believe that you had no help from your master, till I told him seriously that you had not only no master in the house, but that also there was no man in it that had not more need of your help in writing than you of his."

Indeed a good father and a good teacher made the household the wonder of learned Europe. See what More wrote to the tutor he had chosen, when he was himself abroad on an embassy:—

"I have received, my dear Gunnel, your letters, such as they are wont to be, full of elegance and affection. Your love for my children I gather from your letters; their diligence from their own. I rejoice that little Elizabeth has shown as much modesty of deportment in her mother's absence as she could have done in her presence. Tell her that this delights me above all things; for, much as I esteem learning, which, when joined with virtue, is worth all the treasures of kings, what doth the fame of great scholarship, apart from well-regulated conduct, bring us, except distinguished infamy? Especially in women, whom men are ready enough to assail for their knowledge, because it is uncommon and casts a reproach on their own sluggishness. Among other notable benefits which solid learning bestows, I reckon this among the first, that we acquire it not for the mere sake of praise or the esteem of learned men, but for its own true value and use. Thus have I spoken, my Gunnel, somewhat the more in respect of not coveting vainglory, because of those words in your letter wherein you deem that the high quality of Margaret's wit is not to be depressed, which, indeed, is mine own opinion; but I think that they the most truly depress and affront their wit who accustom themselves to practise it on vain and base objects, rather than raise their minds by the study and approval of what is good in itself. It mattereth not in harvest-time whether the corn were sown by a man or a woman, and I see not why learning in like manner may not equally agree with both sexes; for by it reason is cultivated, and, as a field, sown with wholesome precepts, which bring forth good fruit. Even if the soil of a woman's brain be of its own nature bad, and apter to bear fern than corn, by which saying men oft terrify women from learning, I am of opinion that a woman's mind is, for that very reason, all the more in need of manure and good husbandry, that the defect of nature may be redressed."

In these letters, and in many like them, there is given the best, and the most authentic picture of the household of the great Chancellor.

Of More himself it is difficult to speak without using language which seems extravagant. His character was so beautiful, his life so simple and so pure, his conscientiousness so complete, his end so heroic, that he stands out among the sordid meannesses of the sixteenth century like a single star in the darkness of the world. Sinful popes and wicked kings, greedy statesmen and timid clergy, who will accept the king's supremacy one day and then burn what once they adored—among these More has no place. His is a steadfast soul, happy in prosperity and triumphant in the furnace of affliction. "O ye holy and humble men of heart, O ye spirits and souls of the righteous, bless ye the Lord: praise Him and magnify Him for ever."

And the position of More in the age of the Reformation is the more remarkable because he belonged so clearly to the new as well as to the old. He was, in the best sense, a Humanist. He was a scholar and a bitter foe of all obscurantism. He fought the battle of Greek, and so gave to England the scholarship of the succeeding generation to which true religion and sound learning owe so great a debt. He could take no part with those who could defend the old faith only with the rusty weapons of a philosophic system which had failed to meet the aspirations of the new age. No one laughed more readily than he at the sallies of Erasmus against ignorant monks and illiterate clergy. *Encomium Moriæ, Epistolæ Obscurorum Virorum*, spoke his sentiments as well as those of their authors. But while he loved the new learning and adopted the new methods, he saw that there remained something among the old things that was priceless and imperishable. It may be that he did not clearly distinguish between the essentials and the mere offshoots of a divine faith. It may be—we should say it must be—that if he had lived a hundred years later, or in our own day, he would have thought differently on some matters. The cause of intellectual freedom was presented to him in its worst aspect, and the command to cast away the childish things of mediævalism came in a revolting form from the lips of a coarse and brutal tyrant. Had Colet lived, or Erasmus been a stronger man, all might have been different. As it was, More saw but one side of the new world, and that the worst, and he said, "The old is better."

But while, in his final choice, he seemed to belong rather to the old world than to the new, he had absorbed all the best spirit of the Italian Renaissance, and he belonged as a social reformer to an age in the far future. The *Utopia*, it is true, was the work of his youth, and it is doubtful if much of it was meant seriously, and certain that some was distinctly contrary to its author's mature convictions. But nevertheless it sets forth an exquisite ideal picture of equality in opportunity and of simplicity of life. Its whole tone speaks a protest against the selfishness and the competition of the age that degraded art and divided society. And this protest was enforced by the asceticism of the author's own life and the purity of his household.

More's life was not a long one. He was born on February 7, 1478. His family was "honourable, not illustrious." His father came to be an eminent judge. As a boy he went to school in London, and then was taken into the household of the famous Cardinal Morton, Archbishop of Canterbury and Lord High Chancellor of England, the statesman who advised the best measures of Henry VII., who began to reform the monasteries, who heavily taxed the rich and took care for the poor. There the young More was known as a bright lad, who would often speak a piece in Christmas games for the guests' entertainment with a wit and readiness which made the Archbishop prophesy for him a great career. He went to Oxford; he studied at New Inn, and then at Lincoln's Inn. He became a lawyer; he went into Parliament; he lectured publicly in London on theology. When a young man he was widely known as a scholar and a wit. He was a friend of all the learned men of his day, a member of that little circle of students to which Colet and Grocyn and Linacre belonged. Though he plunged into practical life, politics, and law, and exchanged epigrams with the best wits of the time, his deepest thoughts were always with religion. He was near becoming a Carthusian; he had serious thoughts of refraining from marriage; he lived very strictly, and was with difficulty won from a solitary life. When he decided to marry and conform outwardly to the customs of the society of his day, he did not abandon the secret rules by which his personal life was restrained. He was outwardly of the world, but in spirit he was always a recluse.

Gradually he came prominently before his contemporaries. His books made him known to scholars. Wolsey may have known him at Oxford, and now found him useful on embassies and at Court. The King sought him out and made a friend of him, would talk with him of theological matters, obtained his help for that book against Luther which won him the title of "Defender of the Faith," and often at night "would have him up to the leads, there to consider with him the courses, motions, and operations of the stars and planets." So, when Wolsey fell, More, who had already been Speaker of the House of Commons, and won great praise alike from King and Cardinal, became Lord Chancellor—the first great layman and lawyer who held that high office. As judge men spoke of him with admiration for centuries. He was a statesman, too, as well as a lawyer, and his aid was sought in all Henry's foreign negotiations. He might have been the greatest man in England after the King if he would have strained his conscience. But this he would not do. He never approved the Divorce; he was known to be a champion of the injured Queen Katherine, and a friend to her nephew, the Emperor Charles. As Church questions, too, came in dispute, he took more and more the conservative side. He would not repudiate the Pope's supremacy, or separate himself from the imposing unity of Christendom, which it seemed to him was threatened by the nationalism of Henry VIII., as well as by the heresy of Luther. And so at last it came that the lion felt his strength: it was More's own prophecy, and he was one of the first victims.

On Monday, April 13, 1534, he was required to take oath to the succession of the issue of Anne Boleyn, and in repudiation of the validity of the first marriage of the King. He at once refused. He would not deny to swear to the succession, but the oath put before him he could not reconcile with his conscience. In this he persisted. Imprisonment, trial, death, came naturally and inevitably; and of these Miss Manning, with the letters and memoirs before her, has made the faithful Margaret write as from a full heart.

On Tuesday, July 6, 1535, he was executed on Tower Hill. "He bore in his hands a red cross, and was often seen to cast his eyes towards heaven." He died as he had lived, with saintly calm, and still playing with a gentle humour. "That at least," he said, as he drew aside his beard from the block, "has committed no treason."

The King's wrath did not cease with the execution of his faithful counsellor. Dame Alice More lost all, and had hard stress for the few years that remained to her of life. Happily his son and his daughters had all been married before the troubles came. Margaret's marriage was a happy one. Will Roper was soon weaned from his "Lutheran" fancies, and lived, thirty-four years after his wife, to write an exquisite and pathetic memoir of the great Chancellor. When the tyrant was dead More's family seemed almost sacred in the eyes of the nation. His memory was cherished, and memorials of all kinds poured forth during the years of Mary's reign; and when Elizabeth had been twenty years on the throne Roper died in peace, desiring to be buried with his "dear wife," where his father-in-law "did mind to be buried."

Margaret Roper herself died in 1544, and was buried in Chelsea Church. Her monument is, with the Ropers', in S. Dunstan's, Canterbury. In that ancient city the family of her husband had long dwelt, and the house itself lasted till this century. Of it Miss Manning very prettily wrote:—

"My friend, Mrs. George Frederick Young, who was born in the Ropers' house at Canterbury, tells me that it was of singular antiquity, full of queer nooks, corners, and passages, with a sort of dungeon below, that went by the name of 'Dick's Hole,' the access to which was so dangerous that it at length was forbidden to descend the staircase. The coach-house and harness-room were curiously antique; the chapel had been converted into a laundry, but retained its Gothic windows. At length it became needful to rebuild the house, only the old gateway of which remains. While the workmen were busy, an old gentleman in Canterbury sent to beg Mrs. Young's father to dig in a particular part of the garden, for that he had dreamed there was a money-chest there. This request was not attended to, and he sent a more urgent message, saying his dream had been repeated. A third time he dreamed, and renewed his request, which at length was granted; and, curiously enough, a chest *was* found, with a few coins in it, chiefly of antiquarian value, which, accordingly, were given to an archæologist of the place. Here my information ceases."

More and his favourite daughter are those of whom we first think when we try to recall some memories of the "Christian academy;" but their famous guests must not be forgotten. I cannot speak now of the soldiers and diplomatists, the priests and scholars, who pass across the scene so rapidly as we read the letters of the Chancellor himself or the memoirs of his son-in-law and his great-grandson. But two names stand out as famous above the rest, and as both among the closest of those friends whom More delighted to honour,—Erasmus the scholar and Holbein the painter.

Of Erasmus who shall speak in a few words? Are not the libraries of Europe full of his books, and are not his witticisms still repeated to-day as if they were but the new thoughts of the newest of moderns? The intellectual life of his age seems summed up in his person. It had no interest in which he did not mingle, nor any opinion which he did not weigh and test. If he held himself above its passions, it was simply because his was a keen critical nature, loving in its own fashion, but too cold to sympathise deeply with any combatant or to thrill with any passion. "He had no mind," said Miss Manning rather sharply, "to be a martyr, but only to suggest doubts which led braver men to be such."

"This worthy man," says his eighteenth century biographer, Jortin, "spent a laborious life in an uniform pursuit of two points: in opposing barbarous ignorance and blind superstition, and in promoting useful literature and true piety. These objects he attempted in a mild, gentle manner, never attacking the persons of men, but only the faults of the age. He knew his own temper and talents, and was conscious he was not fitted for the rough work of a reformer."

Jortin's, indeed, is the juster estimate. It was Erasmus's keen sight, not his want of moral courage, which prevented his being a martyr. He could not sympathise with the foreign reformers; he had no taste for antinomianism, still less for ignorance, and he saw that the Church abroad, with all its accretions,—which none ridiculed so wittily as he,—still preserved a treasure that the human mind could not afford to lose.

Erasmus was a lifelong friend of More. They had met originally in England while Henry VII. was still on the throne. Erasmus stayed at More's house, and together they discussed the wrongs and follies of the time. *Encomium Moriæ*—"The Praise of Folly"—was written by Erasmus under More's roof, and the title had a punning reference to the author's host. Later books, especially the great edition of the New Testament which made the sacred text, said More, "shine with a new light," had all of them the sanction of the faithful English friend. He had to suffer rough handling from the obscurantists of his day. Greek seemed to savour of heresy, just as now to some it seems a relic of mediævalism unworthy of the study of a scientific age. Erasmus, indeed, was in a position which has its parallel to-day. He stood boldly forth to fight for a large and liberal education, and for wide and rational methods of instruction, against those who would narrow the teaching of the young to a merely technical and professional training. He fought against the effort to sacrifice sound learning to utilitarian ends; and he found the warmest sympathy, and the best expression of his educational ideal, in the household of his English friend.

With More he bore reproach for a good cause. While the English lawyer pleaded for the study of Greek at the English universities, the Dutch scholar met the assaults of those who would check the publication of the New Testament in the original tongue. He was justly indignant at the treatment he received.

"There are none," he said, "that bark at me more furiously than those who have never even seen the outside of my books. When you meet with one of these brawlers, let him rave on at my New Testament till he has made himself hoarse. Then ask him gently whether he has read it. If he has the impudence to say yes, urge him to produce one passage that deserves to be blamed. You will find that he cannot. Consider, now, whether this be the behaviour of a Christian, to blacken a man's reputation, which he cannot restore to him again if he would. Of all the vile ways of defaming him, none is more villainous than to accuse him of heresy; and yet to this they have recourse on the slightest provocation!"

A Dominican friar at Strasburg, who had spitefully attacked Erasmus's Testament, was compelled to own that he had not read one word of it. "These men," exclaims Erasmus, "first hate, next condemn, and, lastly, seek for passages to justify their censures. And then, if any one opposes them, and calls them what they are, they say he is a disturber of the public peace; which is just as if you gave a man a blow in the face, and then bid him be quiet, and not make a noise about nothing."

But all through the babel of contending voices Erasmus kept his own course. He could neither be coerced to give up his liberal scholarship nor lured to ally with Luther and the Protestant doctors. To him the way of sound learning seemed the path of the Catholic Church. And here too he was of one mind with More. The Englishman had to meet dangers which never beset the foreign scholar, and he met them, it may be, as Erasmus would not have dared to do. But it cannot be doubted that in their opinions, as in their hearts, they were never really divided.

In Mistress Margaret's *Libellus*, Erasmus appears chiefly as a fellow of infinite jest, but wise withal, chatting at table as he chats in his letters, and saying, indeed, much that we have under the safe warrant of his own pen.

If Erasmus was the typical scholar of that age which stood between the Renaissance and the Reformation, Hans Holbein was typical of its art. In his hand painting has come down from its high estate, its Madonnas and its great Doges, its classic pageants and its heroic legends, and treats of common life as men saw it every day. The German artist descended from the lofty themes which had inspired the great master of Italy, and took even the humbler work of illustrating books. Botticelli, it is true, had drawn studies of the *Divina Commedia*, but Holbein was ready to work for a printer, and to design letters and tail-pieces for the *Libelli* of his friends. It was through Froben, the great Basle painter, no doubt, that More and Erasmus and Holbein first came together. Holbein illustrated the *Utopia*, and came to England with an introduction from the author of the *Encomium Moriæ*. He was thirty years younger than the Dutch scholar, and twenty years younger than More, but they became his chiefest friends. He tarried some while in More's house, and it was there that he drew some of those marvellous sketches now preserved at Windsor, that give us our truest knowledge of the Court of Henry VIII. Fisher and Warham, the Earl of Surrey and Sir Nicholas Poins, Colet and Godsalve, each in their way representative of a class, but keenly individual and vigorously characteristic, are preserved for us by those few sharp, bold strokes with a power and reality which no portrait-painter has ever surpassed. The luxury and the meanness, the treachery and the cold selfishness, that form the background of the great struggles of the sixteenth century are expressed for all time in those master-sketches which Holbein drew and Margaret Roper, it may be, often looked upon.

And for More's own household we have, besides the letters and the memoirs, the very form and pressure from the great artist's own hand. The original design for the famous picture of the patriarchal family, the three generations living together in love and reverence in their "Platonic Academy," is at Basle; but in England, at Nostell and at Cokethorpe, we have very fair presentments of the great picture as it must have been. More sits by his shrewd old father in his habit as he lived. The gentle, delicate son stands by, book in hand, and near his affianced bride. The stepmother sits stately at one side of the group, and the daughters cluster around. The sorrowful eyes of the great Chancellor, and his pensive, meditative brow, speaking sound conscience and a firm resolve, are not lightly to be forgotten; and the plain, homely face of Margaret Roper, refined and thoughtful through all its solid strength, may well linger in the memories of those who know her beautiful life.

To the number of these Miss Manning's book has added many. She teaches others to love her heroes because she loved them herself. Erasmus and More and Holbein, Gunnel and Clement, Will Roper and faithful Patteson, she knew as if she had lived among them. These, and such as these, are the characters of whom she so skilfully drew portraits which were much more than the fictions of imagination. She wrote from a considerable knowledge of the literature of the time, and with a genuine love of all things beautiful and good. In her style she imitated the quaintness of old English without any precise restriction to the period of Henry VIII.; and in the same way the vocabulary and the spelling which she adopted were not claimed by her as minutely accurate. Over her book and her characters I would gladly linger. But the first speaks for itself, and my office is only to direct readers to it; and for the characters, what I can say is said in my own Life of the great Chancellor and Saint himself, the father of the gentle Margaret whom Miss Manning so happily drew.

But there is a special feature in this reprint of which I must needs say a word. Mr. Herbert Railton and Mr. John Jellicoe show that they too are skilled in the drawing of imaginary portraits—that they have seen More's house as indeed we think it must have been, and his family in their habits as they lived. As the barge brings us past old London Bridge to the Chelsea stairs, the mansion of the Chancellor stands before us in the warm sun as when Ellis Heywood saw it three centuries and a half ago. The children play in the garden, the Jew tells his story, the peacocks flaunt their gay colours, and More reads his old books and cracks his jests, as if the old time had come back again. Bright pictures indeed, and a worthy setting; and the old story is told anew as More himself and Holbein might have loved to think of it. But good wines need no bush, and good pictures no prologue.

W. H. HUTTON.

THE GREAT HOUSE, BURFORD,

July 9, 1895.

SIR THOMAS MORE'S HOUSE.
Drawn by Herbert Railton

THE HOUSEHOLD OF SIR THOMAS MORE

Chelsea, June 18th.

On asking Mr. *Gunnel* to what Use I should put this fayr *Libellus*, he did suggest my making it a Kinde of family Register, wherein to note the more important of our domestick Passages, whether of Joy or Griefe—my Father's Journies and Absences—the Visits of learned Men, theire notable Sayings, etc. "You are ready at the Pen, Mistress *Margaret*," he was pleased to say; "and I woulde humblie advise your journalling in the same fearless Manner in the which you framed that Letter which soe well pleased the *Bishop of Exeter*, that he sent you a Portugal Piece. 'Twill be well to write it in English, which 'tis expedient for you not altogether to negleckt, even for the more honourable Latin."

Methinks I am close upon Womanhood.... "Humblie advise," quotha! to me, that have so oft humblie sued for his Pardon, and sometimes in vayn!

'Tis well to make trial of *Gonellus* his "humble" Advice: albeit, our daylie Course is so methodicall, that 'twill afford scant Subject for the Pen—*Vitam continet una Dies.*

... As I traced the last Word, methoughte I heard the well-known Tones of *Erasmus* his pleasant Voyce; and, looking forthe of my Lattice, did indeede beholde the deare little Man coming up from the River Side with my Father, who, because of the Heat, had given his Cloak to a tall Stripling behind him to bear. I flew up Stairs, to advertise Mother, who was half in and half out of her grogram Gown, and who stayed me to clasp her Owches; so that, by the Time I had followed her down Stairs, we founde 'em alreadie in the Hall.

So soon as I had kissed their Hands, and obtayned their Blessings, the tall Lad stept forthe, and who should he be but *William Roper*, returned from my Father's Errand over-seas! He hath grown hugelie, and looks mannish; but his Manners are worsened insteade of bettered by forayn Travell; for, insteade of his old Franknesse, he hung upon Hand till *Father* bade him come forward; and then, as he went his Rounds, kissing one after another, stopt short when he came to me, twice made as though he would have saluted me, and then held back, making me looke so stupid, that I could have boxed his Ears for his Payns. 'Speciallie as *Father* burst out a-laughing, and cried, "The third Time's lucky!"

After Supper, we took deare *Erasmus* entirely over the House, in a Kind of family Procession, e'en from the Buttery and Scalding-house to our own deare *Academia*, with its cool green Curtain flapping in the Evening Breeze, and blowing aside, as though on Purpose to give a glimpse of the cleare-shining *Thames*!

Erasmus noted and admired the Stone Jar, placed by *Mercy Giggs* on the Table, full of blue and yellow Irises, scarlet Tiger-Lilies, Dog-Roses, Honeysuckles, Moonwort, and Herb-Trinity; and alsoe our various Desks, eache in its own little Retirement,—mine own, in speciall, so pleasantly situate! He protested, with everie Semblance of Sincerity, he had never seene so pretty an Academy. I should think not, indeede! *Bess*, *Daisy*, and I, are of Opinion, that there is not likelie to be such another in the World. He glanced, too, at the Books on our Desks; *Bessy's* being *Livy*; *Daisy's*, *Sallust*; and mine, St. *Augustine*, with *Father's* Marks where I was to read, and where desist. He tolde *Erasmus*, laying his Hand fondlie on my Head, "Here is one who knows what is implied in the Word Trust." Dear *Father*, well I may! He added, "there was no Law against laughing in *his Academia*, for that his Girls knew how to be merry and wise."

From the House to the new Building, the Chapel and Gallery, and thence to visitt all the dumb Kinde, from the great horned Owls to *Cecy's* pet Dormice. *Erasmus* was amused at some of theire Names, but doubted whether *Duns Scotus* and the *Venerable Bede* would have thoughte themselves complimented in being made Name-fathers to a couple of Owls; though he admitted that *Argus* and *Juno* were goode Cognomens for Peacocks. *Will Roper* hath broughte Mother a pretty little forayn Animal called a Marmot, but she sayd she had noe Time for suchlike Playthings, and bade him give it to his little Wife. Methinks, I being neare sixteen and he close upon twenty, we are too old for those childish Names now, nor am I much flattered at a Present not intended for me; however, I shall be kind to the little Creature, and, perhaps, grow fond of it, as 'tis both harmlesse and diverting.

ERASMUS AND THE PEACOCKS.
Drawn by John Jellicoe

To return, howbeit, to *Erasmus*; *Cecy*, who had hold of his Gown, and had al-readie, through his familiar Kindnesse and her own childish Heedlessness, some-what transgrest Bounds, began now in her Mirthe to fabricate a Dialogue, she pretended to have overhearde, between *Argus* and *Juno* as they stoode pearcht on a stone Parapet. *Erasmus* was entertayned with her Garrulitie for a while, but at length gentlie checkt her, with "Love the Truth, little Mayd, love the Truth, or, if thou liest, let it be with a Circumstance," a Qualification which made *Mother* stare and *Father* laugh.

Sayth *Erasmus*, "There is no Harm in a Fabella, Apologus, or Parabola, so long as its Character be distinctlie recognised for such, but contrariwise, much Goode; and the same hath been sanctioned, not only by the wiser Heads of *Greece* and *Rome*, but by our deare Lord Himself. Therefore, *Cecilie*, whom I love exceedinglie, be not abasht, Child, at my Reproof, for thy Dialogue between the two Peacocks was innocent no less than ingenious, till thou wouldst have insisted that they, in sooth, sayd Something like what thou didst invent. Therein thou didst Violence to the Truth, which St. *Paul* hath typified by a Girdle, to be worn next the Heart, and that not only confineth within due Limits, but addeth Strength. So now be Friends; wert thou more than eleven and I no Priest, thou shouldst be my little Wife, and darn my Hose, and make me sweet Marchpane, such as thou and I love. But, oh! this pretty *Chelsea*! What Daisies! what Buttercups! what joviall Swarms of Gnats! The Country all about is as nice and flat as *Rotterdam*."

Anon, we sit down to rest and talk in the Pavilion.

Sayth *Erasmus* to my *Father*, "I marvel you have never entered into the King's Service in some publick Capacitie, wherein your Learning and Knowledge, bothe of Men and Things, would not onlie serve your own Interest, but that of your Friends and the Publick."

Father smiled and made Answer, "I am better and happier as I am. As for my Friends, I alreadie do for them alle I can, soe as they can hardlie consider me in their Debt; and, for myself, the yielding to theire Solicitations that I would putt myself forward for the Benefit of the World in generall, would be like printing a Book at Request of Friends, that the Publick may be charmed with what, in Fact, it values at a Doit. The Cardinall offered me a Pension, as retaining Fee to the King a little while back, but I tolde him I did not care to be a mathematical Point, to have Position without Magnitude."

Erasmus laught and sayd, "I woulde not have you the Slave of anie King; howbeit, you mighte assist him and be useful to him."

"The Change of the Word," sayth *Father*, "does not alter the Matter; I should *be* a Slave, as completely as if I had a Collar rounde my Neck."

"But would not increased Usefulnesse," says *Erasmus*, "make you happier?"

"Happier?" says *Father*, somewhat heating; "how can that be compassed in a Way so abhorrent to my Genius? At present, I live as I will, to which very few Courtiers can pretend. Half-a-dozen blue-coated Serving-Men answer my Turn in the House, Garden, Field, and on the River: I have a few strong Horses for Work, none for Show, plenty of plain Food for a healthy Family, and enough, with a hearty Welcome, for a score of Guests that are not dainty. The lengthe of my Wife's Train infringeth not the Statute; and, for myself, I soe hate Bravery, that my Motto is, 'Of those whom you see in Scarlet, not one is happy.' I have a regular Profession, which supports my House, and enables me to promote Peace and Justice; I have Leisure to chat with my Wife, and sport with my Children; I have Hours for Devotion, and Hours for Philosophie and the liberall Arts, which are absolutelie medicinall to me, as Antidotes to the sharpe but contracted Habitts of Mind engendered by the Law. If there be aniething in a Court Life which can compensate for the Losse of anie of these Blessings, deare *Desiderius*, pray tell me what it is, for I confesse I know not."

"You are a comicall Genius," says *Erasmus*.

"As for you," retorted *Father*, "you are at your olde Trick of arguing on the wrong Side, as you did the firste Time we mett. Nay, don't we know you can declaime backward and forwarde on the same Argument, as you did on the *Venetian War?"*

Erasmus smiled quietlie, and sayd, "What coulde I do? The *Pope* changed his holy Mind." Whereat *Father* smiled too.

"What Nonsense you learned Men sometimes talk!" pursues *Father*. "I—wanted at Court, quotha! Fancy a dozen starving Men with one roasted Pig betweene them;—do you think thcy would be really glad to see a Thirteenth come up, with an eye to a small Piece of the Crackling? No; believe me, there is none that Courtiers are more sincerelie respectfull to than the Man who avows he hath no Intention of attempting to go Shares; and e'en him they care mighty little about, for they love none with true Tendernesse save themselves."

"We shall see you at Court yet," says *Erasmus*.

Sayth *Father*, "Then I will tell you in what Guise. With a Fool's Cap and Bells. Pish! I won't aggravate you, Churchman as you are, by alluding to the Blessings I have which you have not; and I trow there is as much Danger in taking you for serious when you are onlie playful and ironicall as if you were *Plato* himself."

Sayth *Erasmus*, after some Minutes' Silence, "I know full well that you holde *Plato*, in manie Instances, to be sporting when I accept him in very Deed and Truth. *Speculating* he often was; as a brighte, pure Flame must needs be struggling up, and, if it findeth no direct Vent, come forthe of the Oven's Mouth. He was like a Man shut into a Vault, running hither and thither, with his poor, flickering Taper, agonizing to get forthe, and holding himself in readinesse to make a Spring forward the Moment a Door should open. But it never did. 'Not manie Wise are called.' He had clomb a Hill in the Darke, and stoode calling to his Companions below, 'Come on, come on! this Way lies the East; I am avised we shall see the Sun rise anon.' But they never did. What a Christian he woulde have made! Ah! he is one now. He and *Socrates*—the Veil long removed from their Eyes—are sitting at *Jesus'* Feet. *Sancte Socrates, ora pro nobis!"*

Bessie and I exchanged Glances at this so strange Ejaculation; but the Subjeckt was of such Interest, that we listened with deep Attention to what followed.

Sayth *Father*, "Whether *Socrates* were what *Plato* painted him in his Dialogues, is with me a great Matter of Doubte; but it is not of Moment. When so many Contemporaries coulde distinguishe the fancifulle from the fictitious, *Plato's* Object could never have beene to *deceive*. There is something higher in Art than gross Imitation. He who attempteth it is always the leaste successfull; and his Failure hath the Odium of a discovered Lie; whereas, to give an avowedlie fabulous Narrative a Consistence within itselfe which permitts the Reader to be, for the Time, voluntarilie deceived, is as artfulle as it is allowable. Were I to construct a Tale, I woulde, as you sayd to *Cecy*, lie with a Circumstance, but shoulde consider it noe Compliment to have my Unicorns and Hippogriffs taken for live Animals. *Amicus Plato, amicus Socrates, magis tamen amica Veritas.* Now, *Plato* had a much higher Aim than to give a very Pattern of *Socrates* his snub Nose. He wanted a Peg to hang his Thoughts upon——"

"A Peg? A Statue by *Phidias*," interrupts *Erasmus*.

"A Statue by *Phidias*, to clothe in the most beautiful Drapery," sayth *Father*; "no Matter that the Drapery was his own, he wanted to show it to the best Advantage, and to the Honour rather than Prejudice of the Statue. And, having clothed the same, he got a Spark of *Prometheus* his Fire, and made the aforesayd Statue walk and talk, to the Glory of Gods and Men, and sate himself quietlie down in a Corner. By the Way, *Desiderius*, why shouldst thou not submitt thy Subtletie to the Rules of a Colloquy? Set *Eckius* and *Martin Luther* by the Ears! Ha! Man, what Sport! Heavens! if I were to compound a Tale or a Dialogue, what Crotchets and Quips of mine own woulde I not putt into my Puppets' Mouths! and then have out my Laugh behind my Vizard, as when we used to act Burlesques before *Cardinall Morton*. What rare Sporte we had, one Christmas, with a Mummery we called the 'Triall of Feasting'! *Dinner* and *Supper* were broughte up before my *Lord Chief Justice*, charged with Murder. Theire Accomplices were *Plum-pudding, Mince-pye, Surfeit, Drunkenness*, and suchlike. Being condemned to hang by the Neck, I, who was *Supper*, stuft out with I cannot tell you how manie Pillows, began to call lustilie for a Confessor, and, on his stepping forthe, commenct a List of all the Fitts, Convulsions, Spasms, Payns in the Head, and so forthe, I had inflicted on this one and t'other. 'Alas! good Father,' says I, '*King John* layd his Death at my Door;—indeede, there's scarce a royall or noble House that hath not a Charge agaynst me; and I'm sorelie afrayd' (giving a Poke at a fat Priest that sate at my *Lord Cardinall's* Elbow) 'I shall have the Death of *that* holy Man to answer for.'"

Erasmus laughed, and sayd, "Did I ever tell you of the retort of *Willibald Pirkheimer*? A Monk, hearing him praise me somewhat lavishly to another, could not avoid expressing by his Looks great Disgust and Dissatisfaction; and, on being askt whence they arose, confest he could not, with Patience, heare the Commendation of a Man soe notoriously fond of eating Fowls. 'Does he steal them?' says *Pirkheimer*. 'Surely no,' says the Monk. 'Why, then,' quoth *Willibald*, 'I know of a Fox who is ten times the greater Rogue; for, look you, he helps himself to many a fat Hen from my Roost without ever offering to pay me. But tell me now, dear Father, is it then a Sin to eat Fowls?' 'Most assuredlie it is,' says the Monk, 'if you indulge in them to Gluttony.' 'Ah! if, if!' quoth *Pirkheimer*. 'If stands stiff, as the *Lacedemonians* told *Philip* of *Macedon*; and 'tis not by eating Bread alone, my dear Father, you have acquired that huge Paunch of yours. I fancy, if all the fat Fowls that have gone into it could raise their Voices and cackle at once, they woulde make Noise enow to drown the Drums and Trumpets of an army.' Well may *Luther* say," continued *Erasmus*, laughing, "that theire fasting is easier to them than our eating to us; seeing that every Man Jack of them hath to his Evening Meal two Quarts of Beer, a Quart of Wine, and as manie as he can eat of Spice Cakes, the better to relish his Drink. While I ... 'tis true my Stomach is Lutheran, but my Heart is Catholic; that's as Heaven made me, and I'll be judged by you alle, whether I am not as thin as a Weasel."

'Twas now growing dusk, and *Cecy's* tame Hares were just beginning to be on the alert, skipping across our Path, as we returned towards the House, jumping over one another, and raysing 'emselves on theire hind Legs to solicitt our Notice.

Erasmus was amused at theire Gambols, and at our making them beg for Vine-tendrils; and *Father* told him there was hardlie a Member of the Householde who had not a dumb Pet of some Sort. "I encourage the Taste in them," he sayd, "not onlie because it fosters Humanitie and affords harmlesse Recreation, but because it promotes Habitts of Forethoughte and Regularitie. No Child or Servant of mine hath Liberty to adopt a Pet which he is too lazy or nice to attend to himself. A little Management may enable even a young Gentlewoman to do this, without soyling her Hands; and to negleckt giving them proper Food at proper Times entayls a Disgrace of which everie one of 'em would be ashamed. But, hark! there is the Vesper-bell."

As we passed under a Pear-tree, *Erasmus* told us, with much Drollerie, of a Piece of boyish Mischief of his, — the Theft of some Pears off a particular Tree, the Fruit of which the Superior of his Convent had meant to reserve to himself. One Morning, *Erasmus* had climbed the Tree, and was feasting to his great Content, when he was aware of the Superior approaching to catch him in the Fact; soe, quickly slid down to the Ground, and made off in the opposite Direction, limping as he went. The Malice of this Act consisted in its being the Counterfeit of the Gait of a poor lame Lay Brother, who was, in fact, smartlie punisht for *Erasmus* his Misdeede. Our Friend mentioned this with a Kinde of Remorse, and observed to my *Father*, — "Men laugh at the Sins of young People and little Children, as if they were little Sins; albeit, the Robbery of an Apple or Cherry-orchard is as much a breaking of the Eighth Commandment as the stealing of a Leg of Mutton from a Butcher's Stall, and ofttimes with far less Excuse. Our Church tells us, indeede, of Venial Sins, such as the Theft of an Apple or a Pin; but, I think," (looking hard at *Cecilie* and *Jack*,) "even the youngest among us could tell how much Sin and Sorrow was brought into the World by stealing an Apple."

At Bedtime, *Bess* and I did agree in wishing that alle learned Men were as apt to unite Pleasure with Profit in theire Talk as *Erasmus*. There be some that can write after the Fashion of Paul, and others preach like unto Apollos; but this, methinketh, is scattering Seed by the Wayside, like the Great Sower.

Tuesday.

'Tis singular, the Love that *Jack* and *Cecy* have for one another; it resembleth that of Twins. *Jack* is not forward at his Booke; on the other Hand, he hath a Resolution of Character which *Cecy* altogether wants. Last Night, when *Erasmus* spake of Children's Sins, I observed her squeeze *Jack's* Hand with alle her Mighte. I know what she was thinking of. Having bothe beene forbidden to approach a favourite Part of the River Bank which had given way from too much Use, one or the other of 'em transgressed, as was proven by the smalle Footprints in the Mud, as well as by a Nosegay of Flowers, that grow not, save by the River; to wit, Purple Loosestrife, Cream-and-codlins, Scorpion-grass, Water Plantain, and the like. Neither of 'em woulde confesse, and *Jack* was, therefore, sentenced to be whipt. As he walked off with Mr. *Drew*, I observed *Cecy* turn soe pale, that I whispered *Father* I was certayn she was guilty. He made Answer, "Never mind, we cannot beat a Girl, and 'twill answer the same Purpose; in flogging him, we flog both." *Jack* bore the firste Stripe or two, I suppose, well enow, but at lengthe we hearde him cry out, on which *Cecy* coulde not forbeare to doe the same, and then stopt bothe her Ears. I expected everie Moment to heare her say, "*Father*, 'twas I;" but no, she had not Courage for that; onlie, when *Jack* came forthe all smirched with Tears, she put her Arm about his Neck, and they walked off together into the Nuttery. Since that Hour, she hath beene more devoted to him than ever, if possible; and he, Boy-like, finds Satisfaction in making her his little Slave. But the Beauty lay in my *Father's* Improvement of the Circumstance. Taking *Cecy* on his Knee that Evening, (for she was not ostensiblie in Disgrace,) he beganne to talk of Atonement and Mediation for Sin, and who it was that bare our Sins for us on the Tree. 'Tis thus he turns the daylie Accidents of our quiet Lives into Lessons of deepe Import, not pedanticallie delivered, *ex cathedrâ*, but welling forthe from a full and fresh Mind.

JACK AND CECY.
Drawn by John Jellicoe

This Morn I had risen before Dawn, being minded to meditate on sundrie Matters before *Bess* was up and doing, she being given to much Talk during her dressing, and made my Way to the Pavilion, where, methought, I should be quiet enow; but beholde! *Father* and *Erasmus* were there before me, in fluent and earneste Discourse. I would have withdrawne, but *Father*, without interrupting his Sentence, puts his Arm rounde me and draweth me to him; soe there I sit, my Head on 's Shoulder, and mine Eyes on *Erasmus* his Face.

From much they spake, and othermuch I guessed, they had beene conversing on the present State of the Church, and how much it needed Renovation.

Erasmus sayd, the Vices of the Clergy and Ignorance of the Vulgar had now come to a Poynt, at the which, a Remedie must be founde, or the whole Fabric would falle to Pieces.

—Sayd, the Revival of Learning seemed appoynted by Heaven for some greate Purpose, 'twas difficulte to say how greate.

—Spake of the new Art of Printing, and its possible Consequents.

—Of the active and fertile Minds at present turning up new Ground and ferreting out old Abuses.

—Of the Abuse of Monachism, and of the evil Lives of Conventualls. In special, of the Fanaticism and Hypocrisie of the Dominicans.

Considered the Evills of the Times such, as that Societie must shortlie, by a vigorous Effort, shake 'em off.

Wondered at the Patience of the Laitie for soe many Generations, but thoughte 'em now waking from theire Sleepe. The People had of late begunne to know theire physickall Power, and to chafe at the Weighte of theire Yoke.

Thoughte the Doctrine of Indulgences altogether bad and false.

Father sayd, that the graduallie increast Severitie of Church Discipline concerning minor Offences had become such as to render Indulgences the needfulle Remedie for Burthens too heavie to be borne.—Condemned a Draconic Code, that visitted even Sins of Discipline with the extream Penaltie. Quoted how ill such excessive Severitie answered in our owne Land, with regard to the Civill Law; twenty Thieves oft hanging together on the same Gibbet, yet Robberie noe Whit abated.

Othermuch to same Purport, the which, if alle set downe, woulde too soon fill my Libellus. At length, unwillinglie brake off, when the Bell rang us to Matins.

At Breakfaste, *William* and *Rupert* were earneste with my *Father* to let 'em row him to *Westminster*, which he was disinclined to, as he was for more Speede, and had promised *Erasmus* an earlie Caste to *Lambeth*; howbeit, he consented that they should pull us up to *Putney* in the Evening, and *William* should have the Stroke-oar. *Erasmus* sayd, he must thank the *Archbishop* for his Present of a Horse; "tho' I'm full faine," he observed, "to believe it a Changeling. He is idle and gluttonish, as thin as a Wasp, and as ugly as Sin. Such a Horse, and such a Rider!"

In the Evening *Will* and *Rupert* had made 'emselves spruce enow, with Nosegays and Ribbons, and we tooke Water bravelie;—*John Harris* in the Stern, playing the Recorder. We had the six-oared Barge; and when *Rupert Allington* was tired of pulling, Mr. *Clement* tooke his Oar; and when *he* wearied, *John Harris* gave over playing the Pipe; but *William* and Mr. *Gunnel* never flagged.

Erasmus was full of his Visitt to the *Archbishop*, who, as usuall, I think, had given him some Money.

"We sate down two hundred to Table," sayth he; "there was Fish, Flesh, and Fowl; but *Wareham* onlie played with his Knife, and drank noe Wine. He was very cheerfulle and accessible; he knows not what Pride is; and yet, of how much mighte he be proude! What Genius! What Erudition! what Kindnesse and Modesty! From *Wareham*, who ever departed in Sorrow?"

Landing at *Fulham*, we had a brave Ramble thro' the Meadows. *Erasmus*, noting the poor Children a gathering the Dandelion and Milk-thistle for the Herb-market, was avised to speak of forayn Herbes and theire Uses, bothe for Food and Medicine.

"For me," says *Father*, "there is manie a Plant I entertayn in my Garden and Paddock which the Fastidious woulde caste forthe. I like to teache my Children the Uses of common Things—to know, for Instance, the Uses of the Flowers and Weeds that grow in our Fields and Hedges. Manie a poor Knave's Pottage woulde be improved, if he were skilled in the Properties of the Burdock and Purple Orchis, Lady's-smock, Brook-lime, and Old Man's Pepper. The Roots of Wild Succory and Water Arrow-head mighte agreeablie change his Lenten Diet; and Glasswort afford him a Pickle for his Mouthfulle of Salt-meat. Then, there are Cresses and Wood-sorrel to his Breakfast, and Salep for his hot evening Mess. For his Medicine, there is Herb-twopence, that will cure a hundred Ills; Camomile, to lull a raging Tooth; and the Juice of Buttercup to cleare his Head by sneezing. Vervain cureth Ague; and Crowfoot affords the leaste painfulle of Blisters. St. *Anthony's* Turnip is an Emetic; Goose-grass sweetens the Blood; Woodruffe is good for the Liver; and Bindweed hath nigh as much Virtue as the forayn Scammony. Pimpernel promoteth Laughter; and Poppy, Sleep: Thyme giveth pleasant Dreams; and an Ashen Branch drives evil Spirits from the Pillow. As for Rosemarie, I lett it run alle over my Garden Walls, not onlie because my Bees love it, but because 'tis the Herb sacred to Remembrance, and, therefore, to Friendship, whence a Sprig of it hath a dumb Language that maketh it the chosen Emblem at our Funeral Wakes, and in our Buriall Grounds. Howbeit, I am a Schoolboy prating in Presence of his Master, for here is *John Clement* at my Elbow, who is the best Botanist and Herbalist of us all."

—Returning Home, the Youths being warmed with rowing, and in high Spiritts, did entertayn themselves and us with manie Jests and Playings upon Words, some of 'em forced enow, yet provocative of Laughing. Afterwards, Mr. *Gunnel* proposed Enigmas and curious Questions. Among others, he woulde know which of the famous Women of Greece or Rome we Maidens would resemble. *Bess* was for *Cornelia*, *Daisy* for *Clelia*, but I for *Damo*, Daughter of *Pythagoras*, which *William Roper* deemed stupid enow, and thoughte I mighte have found as good a Daughter, that had not died a Maid. Sayth *Erasmus*, with his sweet, inexpressible Smile, "Now I will tell you, Lads and Lasses, what manner of Man *I* would be, if I were not *Erasmus*. I woulde step back some few Years of my Life, and be half-way 'twixt thirty and forty; I would be pious and profounde enow for the Church, albeit noe Churchman; I woulde have a blythe, stirring, English Wife, and half-a-dozen merrie Girls and Boys, an English Homestead, neither Hall nor Farm, but betweene both; neare enow to the Citie for Convenience, but away from its Noise. I woulde have a Profession, that gave me some Hours daylie of regular Businesse, that should let Men know my Parts, and court me into Publick Station, for which my Taste made me rather withdrawe. I woulde have such a private Independence, as should enable me to give and lend, rather than beg and borrow. I woulde encourage Mirthe without Buffoonerie, Ease without Negligence; my Habitt and Table shoulde be simple, and for my Looks I woulde be neither tall nor short, fat nor lean, rubicund nor sallow, but of a fayr Skin with blue Eyes, brownish Beard, and a Countenance engaging and attractive, soe that alle of my Companie coulde not choose but love me."

"Why, then, you woulde be *Father* himselfe," cries *Cecy*, clasping his Arm in bothe her Hands with a Kind of Rapture; and, indeede, the Portraiture was soe like, we coulde not but smile at the Resemblance.

Arrived at the Landing, *Father* protested he was wearie with his Ramble; and, his Foot slipping, he wrenched his Ankle, and sate for an Instante on a Barrow, the which one of the Men had left with his Garden-tools, and before he could rise or cry out, *William*, laughing, rolled him up to the House-door; which, considering *Father's* Weight, was much for a Stripling to doe. *Father* sayd the same, and, laying his Hand on *Will's* Shoulder with Kindnesse, cried, "Bless thee, my Boy, but I woulde not have thee overstrayned like *Biton* and *Cleobis*."

MORE IN THE BARROW.
Drawn by John Jellicoe

June 20.

This Morn, hinting to *Bess* that she was lacing herselfe too straitlie, she brisklie replyed, "One would think 'twere as great Meritt to have a thick Waiste as to be one of the earlie Christians!"

These humourous Retorts are ever at her Tongue's end; and albeit, as *Jacky* one Day angrilie remarked when she had beene teazing him, "*Bess*, thy Witt is Stupidnesse;" yet, for one who talks soe much at Random, no one can be more keene when she chooseth. *Father* sayd of her, half fondly, half apologeticallie, to *Erasmus*, "Her Wit hath a fine Subtletie that eludes you almoste before you have Time to recognize it for what it really is." To which *Erasmus* readilie assented, adding, that it had the rare Meritt of playing less on Persons than Things, and never on bodilie Defects.

Hum!—I wonder if they ever sayd as much in Favour of me. I know, indeede, *Erasmus* calls me a forward Girl. Alas! that may be taken in two Senses.

Grievous Work, overnighte, with the churning. Nought would persuade *Gillian* but that the Creame was bewitched by *Gammer Gurney*, who was dissatisfyde last Friday with her Dole, and hobbled away mumping and cursing. At alle Events, the Butter would not come; but *Mother* was resolute not to have soe much good Creame wasted; soe sent for *Bess* and me, *Daisy* and *Mercy Giggs*; and insisted on our churning in turn till the Butter came, if we sate up alle Night for 't. 'Twas a hard Saying; and mighte have hampered her like as *Jephtha* his rash Vow: howbeit, soe soone as she had left us, we turned it into a Frolick, and sang *Chevy Chase* from end to end, to beguile Time; ne'erthelesse, the Butter would not come; soe then we grew sober, and, at the Instance of sweete *Mercy*, chaunted the 119th Psalme; and, by the Time we had attained to "*Lucerna Pedibus*," I hearde the Buttermilk separating and splashing in righte earneste. 'Twas neare Midnighte, however; and *Daisy* had fallen asleep on the Dresser. *Gillian* will ne'er be convinced but that our Latin brake the Spell.

21st.

Erasmus went to *Richmond* this Morning with *Polus*, (for soe he Latinizes *Reginald Pole*, after his usual Fashion,) and some other of his Friends. On his Return, he made us laugh at the following. They had clomb the Hill, and were admiring the Prospect, when *Pole*, casting his Eyes aloft, and beginning to make sundrie Gesticulations, exclaimed, "What is it I beholde? May Heaven avert the Omen!" with suchlike Exclamations, which raised the Curiositie of alle. "Don't you beholde," cries he, "that enormous Dragon flying through the Sky? his Horns of Fire? his curly Tail?"

"No," says *Erasmus*, "nothing like it. The Sky is as cleare as unwritten Paper."

Howbeit, he continued to affirme and to stare, untill at lengthe, one after another, by dint of strayning theire Eyes and theire Imaginations, did admitt, first, that they saw Something; next, that it mighte be a Dragon; and last, that it was. Of course, on theire Passage homeward, they could talk of little else—some made serious Reflections; others, philosophicall Speculations; and *Pole* waggishly triumphed in having beene the Firste to discerne the Spectacle.

"And you trulie believe there was a Signe in the Heavens?" we inquired of *Erasmus*.

"What know I?" returned he smiling; "you know, *Constantine* saw a Cross. Why shoulde *Polus* not see a Dragon? We must judge by the Event. Perhaps its Mission may be to fly away with *him*. He swore to the curly Tail."

How difficulte it is to discerne the supernatural from the incredible! We laughe at *Gillian's* Faith in our Latin; *Erasmus* laughs at *Polus* his Dragon. Have we a righte to believe noughte but what we can see or prove? Nay, that will never doe. *Father* says a Capacitie for reasoning increaseth a Capacitie for believing. He believes there is such a Thing as Witchcraft, though not that poore olde *Gammer Gurney* is a Witch; he believes that Saints can work Miracles, though not in alle the Marvels reported of the *Canterbury* Shrine.

Had I beene Justice of the Peace, like the King's Grandmother, I would have beene very jealous of Accusations of Witchcraft; and have taken infinite Payns to sift out the Causes of Malice, Jealousie, &c., which mighte have wroughte with the poore olde Women's Enemies. *Holie Writ* sayth, "Thou shalt not suffer a Witch to live;" but, questionlesse, manie have suffered Hurte that were noe Witches; and for my Part, I have alwaies helde ducking to be a very uncertayn as well as very cruel Teste.

I cannot helpe smiling, whenever I think of my Rencounter with *William* this Morning. Mr. *Gunnell* had set me *Homer's* tiresome List of Ships; and, because of the excessive Heate within Doors, I took my Book into the Nuttery, to be beyonde the Wrath of far-darting *Phœbus Apollo*, where I clomb into my favourite Filbert Seat. Anon comes *William* through the Trees without seeing me; and seats him at the Foot of my Filbert; then, out with his Tablets, and, in a Posture I should have called studdied, had he known anie one within Sighte, falls a poetizing, I question not. Having noe Mind to be interrupted, I lett him be, thinking he would soone exhaust the Vein; but a Caterpillar dropping from the Leaves on to my Page, I was fayn, for Mirthe sake, to shake it down on his Tablets. As ill Luck would have it, however, the little Reptile onlie fell among his Curls; which soe took me at Vantage that I coulde not helpe hastilie crying, "I beg your Pardon." 'Twas worth a World to see his Start! "Why!" cries he, looking up, "are there indeede *Hamadryads*?" and would have gallanted a little, but I bade him hold down his Head, while that with a Twig I switched off the Caterpillar. Neither coulde forbeare laughing; and then he sued me to step downe, but I was minded to abide where I was. Howbeit, after a Minute's Pause, he sayd, in a grave, kind Tone, "Come, little Wife;" and taking mine Arm steadilie in his Hand, I lost my Balance and was faine to come down whether or noe. We walked for some Time *juxta Fluvium*; and he talked not badlie of his Travels, insomuch as I founde there was really more in him than one would think.

MARGARET IN THE TREE.
Drawn by John Jellicoe

—Was there ever Aniething soe perverse, unluckie, and downrighte disagreeable? We hurried our Afternoone Tasks, to goe on the Water with my *Father*; and, meaning to give Mr. *Gunnel* my *Latin* Traduction, which is in a Booke like unto this, I never knew he had my Journalle insteade, untill that he burst out a laughing. "Soe this is the famous *Libellus*," quoth he.... I never waited for another Word, but snatcht it out of his Hand; which he, for soe strict a Man, bore well enow. I do not believe he could have read a Dozen Lines, and they were towards the Beginning; but I should hugelie like to know which Dozen Lines they were.

Hum! I have a Mind never to write another Word. That will be punishing myselfe, though, insteade of *Gunnel*. And he bade me not take it to Heart like the late *Bishop of Durham*, to whom a like Accident befel, which soe annoyed him that he died of Chagrin. I will never again, howbeit, write Aniething savouring ever soe little of Levitie or Absurditie. The Saints keepe me to it! And, to know it from my Exercise Book, I will henceforthe bind a blue Ribbon round it. Furthermore, I will knit the sayd Ribbon in soe close a Knot, that it shall be worth no one else's Payns to pick it out. Lastlie, and for entire Securitie, I will carry the Same in my Pouch, which will hold bigger Matters than this.

22nd.

This Daye, at Dinner, Mr. *Clement* tooke the Pistoller's Place at the Reading-desk; and, insteade of continuing the Subject in Hand, read a Paraphrase of the 103rde Psalm; the Faithfulnesse and elegant Turne of which, *Erasmus* highlie commended, though he took Exceptions to the Phrase "renewing thy Youth like that of the Phœnix," whose fabulous Story he believed to have beene unknowne to the Psalmist, and, therefore, however poeticall, unfitt to be introduced. A deepe Blush on sweet *Mercy's* Face ledd to the Detection of the Paraphrast, and drew on her some deserved Commendations. *Erasmus*, turning to my *Father*, exclaymed with Animation, "I woulde call this House the Academy of *Plato*, were it not Injustice to compare it to a Place where the usuall Disputations concerning Figures and Numbers were onlie occasionallie intersperst with Disquisitions concerning the moral Virtues." Then, in a graver Mood, he added, "One mighte envie you, but that your precious Privileges are bound up with soe paynfulle Anxieties. How manie Pledges have you given to Fortune!"

"If my Children are to die out of the Course of Nature, before theire Parents," *Father* firmly replyed, "I would rather they died well-instructed than ignorant."

"You remind me," rejoyns *Erasmus*, "of *Phocion*; whose Wife, when he was aboute to drink the fatal Cup, exclaimed, 'Ah, my Husband! you die innocent.' 'And woulde you, my Wife,' he returned, 'have me die guilty?'"

Awhile after, *Gonellus* askt leave to see *Erasmus* his Signet-ring, which he handed down to him. In passing it back, *William*, who was occupyde in carving a Crane, handed it so negligentlie that it felle to the Ground. I never saw such a Face as *Erasmus* made, when 'twas picked out from the Rushes! And yet, ours are renewed almost daylie, which manie think over nice. He took it gingerlie in his faire, Woman-like Hands, and washed and wiped it before he put it on; which escaped not my Step-mother's displeased notice. Indeede, these *Dutchmen* are scrupulouslie cleane, though *Mother* calls 'em swinish, because they will eat raw Sallets; though, for that Matter, *Father* loves Cresses and Ramps. She alsoe mislikes *Erasmus* for eating Cheese and Butter together with his Manchet; or what he calls *Boetram*; and for being, generallie, daintie at his Sizes, which she sayth is an ill Example to soe manie young People, and becometh not one with soe little Money in 's Purse: howbeit, I think 'tis not Nicetie, but a weak Stomach, which makes him loathe our Salt-meat Commons from Michaelmasse to Easter, and eschew Fish of the coarser Sort. He cannot breakfaste on colde Milk, like *Father*, but liketh Furmity a little spiced. At Dinner, he pecks at, rather than eats, Ruffs and Reeves, Lapwings, or anie smalle Birds it may chance; but affects Sweets and Subtilties, and loves a Cup of Wine or Ale, stirred with Rosemary. *Father* never toucheth the Wine-cup but to grace a Guest, and loves Water from the Spring. We growing Girls eat more than either; and *Father* says he loves to see us slice away at the Cob-loaf; it does him goode. What a kind Father he is! I wish my *Step-mother* were as kind. I hate all sneaping and snubbing, flowting, fleering, pinching, nipping, and such-like; it on-lie creates Resentment insteade of Penitence, and lowers the Minde of either Partie. *Gillian* throws a Rolling-pin at the Turnspit's Head, and we call it Low-life; but we looke for such Unmannerlinesse in the Kitchen. A Whip is onlie fit for *Tisiphone*.

As we rose from Table, I noted *Argus* pearcht on the Window-sill, eagerlie watching for his Dinner, which he looketh for as punctuallie as if he could tell the Diall; and to please the good, patient Bird, till the Scullion broughte him his Mess of Garden-stuff, I fetched him some Pulse, which he took from mine Hand, taking good Heede not to hurt me with his sharp Beak. While I was feeding him, *Erasmus* came up, and asked me concerning *Mercy Giggs*; and I tolde him how that she was a friendlesse Orphan, to whom deare *Father* afforded Protection and the run of the House; and tolde him of her Gratitude, her Meekness, her Patience, her Docilitie, her Aptitude for alle goode Works and Alms-deeds; and how, in her little Chamber, she improved eache spare Moment in the Way of Studdy and Prayer. He repeated "Friendlesse? she cannot be called Friendlesse, who hath *More* for her Protector, and his Children for Companions;" and then woulde heare more of her Parents' sad Story. Alsoe, would hear somewhat of *Rupert Allington*, and how *Father* gained his Lawsuit. Alsoe, of *Daisy*, whose Name he tooke to be the true Abbreviation for *Margaret*, but I tolde him how that my Step-sister, and *Mercy*, and I, being all three of a Name, and I being alwaies called *Meg*, we had in Sport given one the Significative of her characteristic Virtue, and the other that of the French *Marguerite*, which may indeed be rendered either Pearl or Daisy. And *Chaucer*, speaking of our English Daisy, saith

"Si douce est la Marguerite."

"I NOTICED ARGUS PEARCHT."
Drawn by Herbert Railton

23rd.

Since the little Wisdom I have Capacitie to acquire, soe oft gives me the Head-ache to Distraction, I marvel not at *Jupiter's* Payn in his Head, when the Goddess of Wisdom sprang therefrom full growne.

This Morn, to quiet the Payn brought on by too busie Application, Mr. *Gun-nel* would have me close my Book and ramble forth with *Cecy* into the Fields. We strolled towards *Walham Greene*; and she was seeking for Shepherd's Purses and Shepherd's Needles, when she came running back to me, looking rather pale. I askt what had scared her, and she made answer that *Gammer Gurney* was coming along the Hedge. I bade her set aside her Feares; and anon we came up with *Gam-mer*, who was pulling at the purple Blossoms of the Deadly Nightshade. I sayd, "*Gammer*, to what Purpose gather that Weed? knowest not 'tis Evill?"

She sayth, mumbling, "What God hath created, that call not thou evill."

"Well, but," quo' I, "'tis Poison."

"Aye, and Medicine too," returns *Gammer*. "I wonder what we poor Souls might come to, if we tooke Nowt for our Ails and Aches but what we could buy o' the Potticary. We've got noe Dr. *Clement*, we poor Folks, to be our Leech o' the Household."

"But hast no Feare," quo' I, "of an Over-dose?"

"There's manie a Doctor," sayth she, with an unpleasant Leer, "that hath given that at first. In Time he gets his Hand in; and I've had a Plenty o' Practice—Thanks to Self and Sister."

"I knew not," quoth I, "that thou hadst a Sister."

"How should ye, Mistress," returns she shortlie, "when ye never comes nigh us? We've grubbed on together this many a Year."

"'Tis soe far," I returned, half ashamed.

"Why, soe it be," answers *Gammer*; "far from Neighbours, far from Church, and far from Priest; howbeit, my old Legs carries me to *your* House o' Fridays; but I know not whether I shall e'er come agayn—the Rye Bread was soe hard last Time; it may serve for young Teeth, and for them as has got none; but mine, you see, are onlie on the *goe*;" and she opened her Mouth with a ghastly Smile. "'Tis not," she added, "that I'm ungratefulle; but thou sees, Mistress, I really *can't* eat Crusts."

After a Moment, I asked, "Where lies your Dwelling?"

GAMMER GURNEY.
Drawn by John Jellicoe

"Out by yonder," quoth she, pointing to a shapeless Mass like a huge Bird's Nest in the Corner of the Field. "There bides poor *Joan* and I. Wilt come and looke within, Mistress, and see how a Christian can die?"

I mutelie complyed, in spite of *Cecy's* pulling at my Skirts. Arrived at the wretched Abode, which had a Hole for its Chimney, and another for Door at once and Window, I found, sitting in a Corner, propped on a Heap of Rushes, dried Leaves, and olde Rags, an aged sick Woman, who seemed to have but a little While to live. A Mug of Water stoode within her Reach; I saw none other Sustenance; but, in her Visage, oh, such Peace!... Whispers *Gammer* with an awfulle Look, "She sees 'em now!"

"Sees who?" quoth I.

"Why, Angels in two long Rows, afore the Throne of GOD, a bending of themselves, this Way, with theire Faces to th' Earth, and Arms stretched out afore 'em."

"Hath she seen a Priest?" quoth I.

"LORD love ye," returns *Gammer*, "what coulde a Priest doe for her? She's in Heaven alreadie. I doubte if she can heare me." And then, in a loud, distinct Voyce, quite free from her usuall Mumping, she beganne to recite in *English*, "Blessed is every one that feareth the LORD, and walketh in his Ways," etc.; which the dying Woman hearde, although alreadie speechlesse; and reaching out her feeble Arm unto her Sister's Neck, she dragged it down till their Faces touched; and then, looking up, pointed at Somewhat she aimed to make her see ... and we alle looked up, but saw Noughte. Howbeit, she pointed up three severall Times, and lay, as it were, transfigured before us, a gazing at some transporting Sighte, and ever and anon turning on her Sister Looks of Love; and, the While we stoode thus agaze, her Spiritt passed away without even a Thrill or a Shudder. *Cecy* and I beganne to weepe; and, after a While, soe did *Gammer*; then, putting us forthe, she sayd, "Goe, Children, goe; 'tis noe goode crying; and yet I'm thankfulle to ye for your Teares."

I sayd, "Is there Aught we can doe for thee?"

She made Answer, "Perhaps you can give me Tuppence, Mistress, to lay on her poor Eyelids and keep 'em down. Bless 'ee, bless 'ee! You're like the good Samaritan—he pulled out Twopence. And maybe, if I come to 'ee To-morrow, you'll give me a Lapfulle of Rosemarie, to lay on her poor Corpse.... I know you've Plenty. GOD be with 'ee, Children; and be sure ye mind how a Christian can die."

Soe we left, and came Home sober enow. *Cecy* sayth, "To die is not soe fearfulle, *Meg*, as I thoughte, but shoulde *you* fancy dying without a Priest? I shoulde not; and yet *Gammer* sayd she wanted not one. Howbeit, for certayn, *Gammer Gurney* is noe Witch, or she would not soe prayse GOD."

To conclude, *Father*, on hearing Alle, hath given *Gammer* more than enow for her present Needes; and *Cecy* and I are the Almoners of his Mercy.

June 24th.

Yesternighte, being *St. John's Eve*, we went into Town to see the mustering of the Watch. Mr. *Rastall* had secured us a Window opposite the *King's Head*, in *Chepe*, where theire Majestys went in State to see the Show. The Streets were a Marvell to see, being like unto a Continuation of fayr Bowres or Arbours, garlanded acrosse and over the Doors with greene Birch, long Fennel, Orpin, St. *John's* Wort, white Lilies, and such like; with innumerable Candles intersperst, the which, being lit up as soon as 'twas Dusk, made the Whole look like enchanted Land; while, at the same Time, the leaping over Bon-fires commenced, and produced Shouts of Laughter. The Youths woulde have had *Father* goe downe and joyn 'em; *Rupert*, speciallie, begged him hard, but he put him off with, "Sirrah, you Goose-cap, dost think 'twoulde befitt the Judge of the *Sheriffs' Court*?"

At length, to the Sound of Trumpets, came marching up *Cheapside* two Thousand of the Watch, in white Fustian, with the City Badge; and seven hundred Cressett Bearers, eache with his Fellow to supplie him with Oyl, and making, with theire flaring Lights, the Night as cleare as Daye. After 'em, the Morris-dancers and City Waites; the Lord Mayor on horseback, very fine, with his Giants and Pageants; and the Sheriff and his Watch, and *his* Giants and Pageants. The Streets very uproarious on our way back to the Barge, but the homeward Passage delicious; the Nighte Ayre cool; and the Stars shining brightly. *Father* and *Erasmus* had some astronomick Talk; howbeit, methoughte *Erasmus* less familiar with the heavenlie Bodies than *Father* is. Afterwards they spake of the King, but not over-freelie, by reason of the Bargemen overhearing. Thence, to the ever-vext Question of *Martin Luther*, of whome *Erasmus* spake in Terms of earneste, yet qualifyde Prayse.

"If *Luther* be innocent," quoth he, "I woulde not run him down by a wicked Faction; if he be in Error, I woulde rather have him reclaymed than destroyed; for this is most agreeable to the Doctrine of our deare Lord and Master, who woulde not bruise the broken Reede, nor quenche the smoking Flax." And much more to same Purpose.

We younger Folks felle to choosing our favourite Mottoes and Devices, in which the Elders at length joyned us. *Mother's* was loyal—"Cleave to the Crown though it hang on a Bush." *Erasmus's* pithie—"*Festina lente.*" *William* sayd he was indebted for his to St. *Paul*—"I seeke not yours, but you." For me, I quoted one I had seene in an olde Countrie Church, "*Mieux être que paroître*," which pleased *Father* and *Erasmus* much.

June 25th.

Poor *Erasmus* caughte colde on the Water last Nighte, and keeps House to-daye, taking warm Possets. 'Tis my Week of Housekeeping under Mother's Guidance, and I never had more Pleasure in it; delighting to suit his Taste in sweete Things, which, methinks, all Men like. I have enow of Time left for Studdy, when alle's done.

He hathe beene the best Part of the Morning in our Academia, looking over Books and Manuscripts, taking Notes of some, discoursing with Mr. *Gunnel* on others; and, in some Sorte, interrupting our Morning's Work; but how pleasantlie! Besides, as *Father* sayth, "Varietie is not always Interruption. That which occasion-allie lets and hinders our accustomed Studdies, may prove to the ingenious noe less profitable than theire Studdies themselves."

They beganne with discussing the Pronunciation of Latin and Greek, on which *Erasmus* differeth much from us, though he holds to our Pronunciation of the *Theta*. Thence, to the absurde Partie of the *Ciceronians* now in *Italie*, who will admit noe Author save *Tully* to be read nor quoted, nor any Word not in his Writings to be used. Thence to the Latinitie of the *Fathers*, of whose Style he spake slightlie enow, but rated *Jerome* above *Augustine*. At length, to his *Greek* and *Latin Testament*, of late issued from the Presse, and the incredible Labour it hath cost him to make it as perfect as possible: on this Subject he so warmed that *Bess* and I listened with suspended Breath. "May it please GOD," sayth he, knitting ferventlie his Hands, "to make it a Blessing to all Christendom! I look for noe other Reward. Scholars and Believers yet unborn may have Reason to thank, and yet may forget *Erasmus*." He then went on to explain to *Gunnel* what he had much felt in want of, and hoped some Scholar might yet undertake; to wit, a Sort of *Index Bibliorum*, showing in how manie Passages of Holy Writ occurreth anie given Word, etc.; and he e'en proposed it to *Gunnel*, saying 'twas onlie the Work of Patience and Industry, and mighte be layd aside, and resumed as Occasion offered, and completed at Leisure, to the great Thankfullenesse of Scholars. But *Gunnel* onlie smiled and shooke his Head. Howbeit, *Erasmus* set forth his Scheme soe playnlie, that I, having a Pen in Hand, did privilie note down alle the Heads of the same, thinking, if none else would undertake it, why should not I? since Leisure and Industrie were alone required, and since 'twoulde be soe acceptable to manie, 'speciallie to *Erasmus*.

June 29th.

Hearde *Mother* say to *Barbara*, "Be sure the Sirloin is well basted for the King's Physician;" which avised me that Dr. *Linacre* was expected. In Truth, he returned with *Father* in the Barge; and they tooke a Turn on the River Bank before sitting down to Table. I noted them from my Lattice; and anon, *Father*, beckoning me, cries, "Child, bring out my favourite Treatyse on Fisshynge, printed by *Wynkyn de Worde*; I must give the Doctor my loved Passage."

Joyning 'em with the Booke, I found *Father* telling him of the Roach, Dace, Chub, Barbel, etc., we oft catch opposite the Church; and hastilie turning over the Leaves, he beginneth with Unction to read the Passage ensuing, which I love to the full as much as he:—

He observeth, if the Angler's Sport shoulde fail him, "he at the best hathe his holsom Walk and mery at his Ease, a swete Ayre of the swete Savour of the Meade of Flowers, that maketh him hungry; he heareth the melodious Harmonie of Fowles, he seeth the young Swans, Herons, Ducks, Cotes, and manie other Fowles, with theire Broods, which me seemeth better than alle the Noise of Hounds, Faukenors, and Fowlers can make. And if the Angler take Fysshe, then there is noe Man merrier than he is in his Spryte." And, "Ye shall not use this foresaid crafty Disporte for no covetysnesse in the encreasing and sparing of your Money onlie, but pryncipallie for your Solace, and to cause the Health of your Bodie, and speciallie of your Soule, for when ye purpose to goe on your Disportes of Fysshynge, ye will not desire greatlie manie Persons with you, which woulde lett you of your Game. And thenne ye may serve GOD devoutlie, in saying affectuouslie your customable Prayer; and thus doing, ye shall eschew and voyd manie Vices."

MORE READING WYNKYN DE WORDE.
Drawn by John Jellicoe and Herbert Railton

"Angling is itselfe a Vice," cries *Erasmus*, from the Thresholde; "for my Part I will fish none, save and except for pickled Oysters."

"In the Regions below," answers *Father*; and then laughinglie tells *Linacre* of his firste Dialogue with *Erasmus*, who had beene feasting in my Lord Mayor's Cellar:—"'Whence come you?' 'From below.' 'What were they about there?' 'Eating live Oysters, and drinking out of Leather Jacks.' 'Either you are *Erasmus*,' etc. 'Either you are *More* or Nothing.'"

"'Neither more nor less,' you should have rejoyned," sayth the Doctor.

"How I wish I had!" says *Father*; "don't torment me with a Jest I might have made and did not make; 'speciallie to put downe *Erasmus*."

"*Concedo nulli*," sayth *Erasmus*.

"Why are you so lazy?" asks *Linacre*; "I am sure you can speak English if you will."

"Soe far from it," sayth *Erasmus*, "that I made my Incapacitie an Excuse for declining an English Rectory. Albeit, you know how *Wareham* requited me; saying, in his kind, generous Way, I served the Church more by my Pen than I coulde by preaching Sermons in a countrie Village."

Sayth *Linacre*, "The Archbishop hath made another Remark, as much to the Purpose: to wit, that he has received from you the Immortalitie which Emperors and Kings cannot bestow."

"They cannot even bid a smoking Sirloin retain its Heat an Hour after it hath left the Fire," sayth *Father*. "Tilly-vally! as my good *Alice* says, — let us remember the universal Doom, '*Fruges consumere nati*,' and philosophize over our Ale and Bracket."

"Not *Cambridge* Ale, neither," sayth *Erasmus*.

"Will you never forget that unlucky Beverage?" sayth *Father*. "Why, Man, think how manie poor Scholars there be, that content themselves, as I have hearde one of St. *John's* declare, with a penny piece of Beef amongst four, stewed into Pottage with a little Salt and Oatmeal; and that after fasting from four o'clock in the Morning! Say Grace for us this Daye, *Erasmus*, with goode Heart."

At Table, Discourse flowed soe thicke and faste that I mighte aim in vayn to chronicle it — and why should I? dwelling as I doe at the Fountayn Head? Onlie that I find Pleasure, alreadie, in glancing over the foregoing Pages whensoever they concern *Father* and *Erasmus*, and wish they were more faithfullie recalled and better writ. One Thing sticks by me, — a funny Reply of *Father's* to a Man who owed him Money and who put him off with "*Memento Morieris*." "I bid you," retorted *Father*, "*Memento Mori Æris*, and I wish you woulde take as goode Care to provide for the one as I do for the other."

Linacre laughed much at this, and sayd, — "That was real Wit; a Spark struck at the Moment; and with noe Ill-nature in it, for I am sure your Debtor coulde not help laughing."

"Not he," quoth *Erasmus*. "*More's* Drollerie is like that of a young Gentlewoman of his Name, which shines without burning," ... and, oddlie enow, he looked acrosse at *me*. I am sure he meant *Bess*.

July 1st.

Father broughte home a strange Guest to-daye, — a converted *Jew*, with grizzlie Beard, furred Gown, and Eyes that shone like Lamps lit in dark Cavernes. He had beene to *Benmarine* and *Tremeçen*, to the *Holie Citie* and to *Damascus*, to *Urmia* and *Assyria*, and I think alle over the knowne World; and tolde us manie strange Tales, one hardlie knew how to believe; as, for Example, of a Sea-coast Tribe, called the *Balouches*, who live on Fish and build theire Dwellings of the Bones. Alsoe, of a Race of his Countriemen beyond *Euphrates* who believe in *Christ*, but know nothing of the Pope; and of whom were the Magians that followed the Star. This agreeth not with our Legend. He averred that, though soe far apart from theire Brethren, theire Speech was the same, and even theire Songs; and he sang or chaunted one which he sayd was common among the Jews alle over the World, and had beene soe ever since theire Citie was ruinated and the People captivated, and yet it was never sett down in Prick-song. *Erasmus*, who knows little or nought of Hebrew, listened to the Words with Curiositie, and made him repeate them twice or thrice: and though I know not the Character, it seemed to me they sounded thus:—

> *Adir Hu yivne bethcha beccaro,*
> *El, b'ne; El, b'ne; El, b'ne;*
> *Bethcha beccaro.*

THE JEW.
Drawn by John Jellicoe

Though Christianish, he woulde not eat Pig's Face; and sayd Swine's Flesh was forbidden by the Hebrew Law for its unwholesomenesse in hot Countries and hot Weather, rather than by way of arbitrarie Prohibition. *Daisy* took a great Dislike to this Man, and woulde not sit next him.

In the Hay-field alle the Evening. Swathed *Father* in a Hay-rope, and made him pay the Fine, which he pretended to resist. *Cecy* was just about to cast one round *Erasmus*, when her Heart failed and she ran away, colouring to the Eyes. He sayd, he never saw such pretty Shame. *Father* reclining on the Hay, with his Head on my Lap and his Eyes shut, *Bess* asked if he were asleep. He made answer, "Yes, and dreaming." I askt, "Of what?" "Of a far-off future Daye, *Meg*; when thou and I shall looke back on this Hour, and this Hay-field, and my Head on thy Lap."

"Nay, but what a stupid Dream, Mr. *More*," says *Mother*. "Why, what woulde *you* dreame of, Mrs. *Alice*?" "Forsooth, if I dreamed at alle, when I was wide awake, it shoulde be of being *Lord Chancellor* at the leaste." "Well, Wife, I forgive thee for not saying at the *most*. Lord Chancellor, quotha! And you woulde be Dame *Alice*, I trow, and ride in a Whirlecote, and keep a Spanish Jennet, and a Couple of Greyhounds, and wear a Train before and behind, and carry a Jerfalcon on your Fist." "On my Wrist." "No, that's not such a pretty Word as t'other! Go to, go!"

Straying from the others, to a remote Corner of the Meadow, or ever I was aware, I came close upon *Gammer Gurney*, holding Somewhat with much Care. "Give ye good den, Mistress *Meg*," quoth she, "I cannot abear to rob the Birds of theire Nests; but I knows you and yours be kind to dumb Creatures, soe here's a Nest o' young Owzels for ye—and I can't call 'em dumb nowther, for they'll sing bravelie some o' these Days." "How hast fared, of late, *Gammer*?" quoth I. "Why, well enow for such as I," she made Answer; "since I lost the Use o' my right Hand, I can nowther spin, nor nurse sick Folk, but I pulls Rushes, and that brings me a few Pence, and I be a good Herbalist; onlie, because I says one or two English Prayers, and hates the Priests, some Folks thinks me a Witch." "But why dost hate the Priests?" quoth I. "Never you mind," she gave Answer, "I've Reasons manie; and for my English Prayers, they were taught me by a Gentleman I nursed, that's now a Saint in Heaven, along with poor *Joan*."

And soe she hobbled off, and I felt kindlie towards her, I scarce knew why—perhaps because she spake soe lovingly of her dead Sister, and because of that Sister's Name. *My* Mother's Name was *Joan*.

July 2nd.

Erasmus is gone. His last Saying to *Father* was, "They will have you at Court yet;" and *Father's* Answer, "When *Plato's* Year comes round."

To me he gave a Copy, how precious! of his Testament. "You are an elegant Latinist, *Margaret*," he was pleased to say, "but, if you woulde drink deeplie of the Well-springs of Wisdom, applie to Greek. The Latins have onlie shallow Rivulets; the Greeks, copious Rivers, running over Sands of Gold. Read *Plato*; he wrote on Marble, with a Diamond; but above alle, read the New Testament. 'Tis the Key to the Kingdom of Heaven."

To Mr. *Gunnel*, he said smiling, "Have a Care of thyself, dear *Gonellus*, and take a little Wine for thy Stomach's Sake. The Wages of most Scholars now-a-days, are weak Eyes, Ill-health, an empty Purse, and shorte Commons. I neede only bid thee beware of the two first."

To *Bess*, "Farewell, *Bessy*; thank you for mending my bad Latin. When I write to you, I will be sure to signe myselfe, '*Roterodamius.*' Farewell, sweete *Cecil*; let me always continue your 'desired Amiable.' And you, *Jacky*,—love your Book a little more."

"*Jack's* deare Mother, not content with her Girls," sayth *Father*, "was alwaies wishing for a Boy, and at last she had one that means to remain a Boy alle his Life."

"The Dutch Schoolmasters thoughte *me* dulle and heavie," sayth *Erasmus*, "soe there is some Hope of *Jacky* yet." And soe, stepped into the Barge, which we watched to *Chelsea Reach*. How dulle the House has beene ever since! *Rupert* and *William* have had me into the Pavillion to hear the Plot of a Miracle-play they have alreadie begunne to talke over for *Christmasse*, but it seemed to me downrighte

Rubbish. *Father* sleepes in Town to-nighte, soe we shall be stupid enow. *Bessy* hath undertaken to work *Father* a Slipper for his tender Foot; and is happie, tracing for the Pattern our three Moorcocks and Colts; but I am idle and tiresome.

If I had Paper, I woulde beginne my projected *Opus*; but I dare not ask *Gunnel* for anie more just yet; nor have anie Money to buy Some. I wish I had a couple of Angels. I think I shall write to *Father* for them to-morrow; he alwaies likes to heare from us if he is twenty-four Hours absent, providing we conclude not with "I have Nothing more to say."

July 4th.

I have writ my Letter to *Father*. I almoste wish, now, that I had not sent it.

Rupert and *Will* still full of theire Moralitie, which reallie has some Fun in it. To ridicule the Extravagance of those who, as the Saying is, carry theire Farms and Fields on theire Backs, *William* proposes to come in, all verdant, with a reall Model of a Farm on his Back, and a Windmill on his Head.

July 5th.

How sweete, how gracious an Answer from *Father*! *John Harris* has broughte me with it the two Angels; less prized than this Epistle.

July 10th.

Sixteenth Birthdaye. *Father* away, which made it sadde. *Mother* gave me a payr of blue Hosen with Silk Clocks; Mr. *Gunnel*, an ivorie-handled Stylus; *Bess*, a Bodkin for my Hair; *Daisy*, a Book-mark; *Mercy*, a Saffron Cake; *Jack*, a Basket; and *Cecil*, a Nosegay. *William's* Present was fayrest of alle, but I am hurte with him and myselfe; for he offered it soe queerlie and tagged it with such ... I refused it, and there's an End. 'Twas unmannerlie and unkinde of me, and I've cried aboute it since.

Father alwaies gives us a Birthdaye Treat; soe, contrived that *Mother* shoulde take us to see my *Lord Cardinal* of *York* goe to *Westminster* in State. We had a merrie Water-partie; got goode Places and saw the Show; Crosse-bearers, Pillar-bearers, Ushers and alle. Himselfe in crimson engrayned Sattin, and Tippet of Sables, with an Orange in his Hand helde to 's Nose, as though the common Ayr were too vile to breathe. What a pompous Priest it is! The Archbishop mighte well say, "That Man is drunk with too much Prosperitie."

THE CARDINAL'S PROCESSION.
Drawn by John Jellicoe

Betweene Dinner and Supper, we had a fine Skirmish in the Straits of Thermopylæ. Mr. *Gunnel* headed the Persians, and *Will* was *Leonidas*, with a swashing Buckler, and a Helmet a Yard high; but Mr. *Gunnel* gave him such a Rap on the Crest that it went over the Wall; soe then *William* thought there was Nothing left for him but to die. Howbeit, as he had beene layd low sooner than he had reckoned on, he prolonged his last Agonies a goode deal, and gave one of the Persians a tremendous Kick just as they were aboute to rifle his Pouch. They therefore thoughte there must be Somewhat in it they shoulde like to see; soe, helde him down in spite of his hitting righte and lefte, and pulled therefrom, among sundrie lesser Matters, a carnation Knot of mine. Poor Varlet, I wish he would not be so stupid.

After Supper, *Mother* proposed a Concert; and we were alle singing a Rounde, when, looking up, I saw *Father* standing in the Door-way, with such a happy Smile on his Face! He was close behind *Rupert* and *Daisy*, who were singing from the same Book, and advertised them of his Coming by gentlie knocking theire Heads together; but I had the firste Kiss, even before *Mother*, because of my Birthdaye.

July 11th.

It turns out that *Father's* Lateness Yester-even was caused by Press of Businesse; a forayn Mission having beene proposed to him, which he resisted as long as he could, but was at length reluctantlie induced to accept. Lengthe of his Stay uncertayn, which casts a Gloom on alle; but there is soe much to doe as to leave little Time to think, and *Father* is busiest of alle; yet hath founde Leisure to concert with Mother for us a Journey into the Country, which will occupy some of the Weeks of his Absence. I am fulle of carefulle Thoughts and Forebodings, being naturallie of too anxious a Disposition. Oh, let me caste alle my Cares on another!

Fecisti nos ad te, Domine; et inquietum est cor nostrum, donec requiescat in te.

May 27th, 1523.

'Tis soe manie Months agone since that I made an Entry in my *Libellus*, as that my Motto, *"Nulla Dies sine Linea,"* hath somewhat of Sarcasm in it. How manie Things doe I beginne and leave unfinisht! and yet, less from Caprice than Lack of Strength; like him of whom the Scripture was writ, —"This Man beganne to build and was not able to finish." My *Opus*, for instance; the which my *Father's* prolonged Absence in the Autumn, and my Winter Visitt to Aunt *Nan* and Aunt *Fan* gave me such Leisure to carrie forward. But alack! Leisure was less to seeke than Learninge; and when I came back to mine olde Taskes, Leisure was awanting too; and then, by reason of my sleeping in a separate Chamber, I was enabled to steale Hours from the earlie Morn and Hours from the Night, and, like unto *Solomon's* virtuous Woman, my Candle went not out. But 'twas not to Purpose that I worked, like the virtuous Woman, for I was following a Jack-o-Lantern; having forsooke the straight Path laid downe by *Erasmus* for a foolish Path of mine owne; and soe I toyled, and blundered, and puzzled, and was mazed; and then came on that Payn in my Head. *Father* sayd, "What makes *Meg* soe pale?" and I sayd not: and, at the last, I tolde *Mother* there was somewhat throbbing and twisting in the Back of mine Head, like unto a little Worm that woulde not die; and she made Answer, "Ah, a Maggot," and soe by her Scoff I was shamed. Then I gave over mine *Opus*, but the Payn did not yet goe; soe then I was longing for the deare Pleasure, and fondlie turning over the Leaves, and wondering woulde *Father* be surprised and pleased with it some Daye, when *Father* himself came in or ever I was aware. He sayth, "What hast thou, *Meg*?" I faltered and woulde sett it aside. He sayth, "Nay, let me see;" and soe takes it from me; and after the firste Glance throws himself into a Seat, his Back to me, and firste runs it hastilie through, then beginnes with Methode and such Silence and Gravitie as that I trembled at his Side, and felt what it must be to stand a Prisoner at the Bar, and he the Judge. Sometimes I thought he must be pleased, at others not: at lengthe, alle my fond Hopes were ended by his crying, "This will never doe. Poor Wretch, hath this then beene thy Toyl? How couldst find Time for soe much Labour? for here hath beene Trouble enow and to spare. Thou must have stolen it, sweet *Meg*, from the Night, and prevented the Morning Watch. Most dear'st! thy *Father's* owne loved Child;" and soe, caressing me till I gave over my Shame and Disappointment.

"I neede not to tell thee, *Meg*," *Father* sayth, "of the unprofitable Labour of *Sisyphus*, nor of drawing Water in a Sieve. There are some Things, most deare one, that a Woman, if she trieth, may doe as well as a Man; and some she cannot, and some she had better not. Now, I tell thee firmlie, since the firste Payn is the leaste sharpe, that, despite the Spiritt and Genius herein shewn, I am avised 'tis Work thou canst not and Work thou hadst better not doe. But judge for thyselfe;

if thou wilt persist, thou shalt have Leisure and Quiet, and a Chamber in my new Building, and alle the Help my Gallery of Books may afford. But thy Father says, Forbear."

Soe, what coulde I say, but "My Father shall never speak to me in vayn."

Then he gathered the Papers up and sayd, "Then I shall take Temptation out of your Way;" and pressing 'em to his Heart as he did soe, sayth, "They are as deare to me as they can be to you;" and soe left me, looking out as though I noted (but I noted not) the cleare-shining *Thames*. 'Twas Twilighte, and I stoode there I know not how long, alone and lonely; with Tears coming, I knew not why, into mine Eyes. There was a Weight in the Ayr, as of coming Thunder; the Screaming, ever and anon, of *Juno* and *Argus*, inclined me to Mellancholie, as it alwaies does: and at length I beganne to note the Moon rising, and the deepening Clearnesse of the Water, and the lazy Motion of the Barges, and the Flashes of Light whene'er the Rowers dipt theire Oars. And then I beganne to attend to the Cries and different Sounds from acrosse the Water, and the Tolling of a distant Bell; and I felle back on mine olde heart-sighinge, "*Fecisti nos ad te, Domine; et inquietum est cor nostrum, donec requiescat in te.*"

Or ever the Week was gone, my Father had contrived for me another Journey to *New Hall*, to abide with the Lay Nuns, as he calleth them, Aunt *Nan* and Aunt *Fan*, whom my Step-mother loveth not, but whom I love and whom *Father* loveth. Indeede, 'tis sayd in *Essex* that at first he inclined to Aunt *Nan* rather than to my Mother; but that, perceiving my Mother affected his Companie and Aunt *Nan* affected it not, he diverted his hesitating Affections unto her and took her to wife. Howbeit, Aunt *Nan* loveth him dearlie as a Sister ought: indeed, she loveth alle, except, methinketh, herself, to whom, alone, she is rigid and severe. How holie are my Aunts' Lives! Cloistered Nuns could not be more pure, and could scarce be as usefulle. Though wise, they can be gay; though noe longer young, they love the Young. And theire Reward is, the Young love them; and I am fulle sure in this World they seek noe better.

Returned to *Chelsea*, I spake much in Prayse of mine Aunts, and of single Life. On a certayn Evening, we Maids were sett at our Needles and Samplers on the Pavilion Steps; and, as Follie will out, 'gan talk of what we would fayn have to our Lots, shoulde a good Fairie starte up and grant eache a Wish. *Daisy* was for a Countess's Degree, with Hawks and Hounds. *Bess* was for founding a College, *Mercy* a Hospital, and she spake soe experimentallie of its Conditions that I was fayn to goe Partners with her in the same. *Cecy* commenced, "Supposing I were married; if once that I were married" — on which, *Father*, who had come up unperceived, burst out laughing and sayth, "Well, Dame *Cecily*, and what State would you keep?" Howbeit, as he and I afterwards paced together, *juxta Fluvium*, he did say, "*Mercy* hath well propounded the Conditions of an Hospital or Alms-house for aged and sick Folk, and 'tis a Fantasie of mine to sett even such an one afoot, and give you the Conduct of the same."

From this careless Speech, dropped as 'twere by the Way, hath sprung mine House of Refuge! and oh, what Pleasure have I derived from it! How good is my

Father! how the Poor bless him! and how kind is he, through them, to me! Laying his Hand kindly on my Shoulder, this Morning, he sayd, "*Meg*, how fares it with thee now? Have I cured the Payn in thy Head?" Then, putting the House-key into mine Hand, he laughingly added, "'Tis now yours, my Joy, by *Livery* and *Seisin*."

Aug. 6th.

I wish *William* would give me back my Testament. 'Tis one thing to steal a Knot or a Posie, and another to borrow the most valuable Book in the House, and keep it Week after Week. He soughte it with a kind of Mysterie, soe as that I forbeare to ask it of him in Companie, lest I should doe him an ill Turn; and yet I have none other Occasion.

Alle Parties are striving which shall have *Erasmus*, and alle in vayn. E'en thus it was with him when he was here last,—the *Queen* would have had him for her Preceptor, the *King* and *Cardinall* prest on him a royall Apartment and Salarie, *Oxford* and *Cambridge* contended for him, but his Saying was, "Alle these I value less than my Libertie, my Studdies, and my literaric Toyls." How much greater is he than those who woulde confer on him Greatnesse! Noe Man of Letters hath equall Reputation, or is soe much courted.

Aug. 7th.

Yester-even, after overlooking the Men playing at Loggats, *Father* and I strayed away along *Thermopylæ* into the Home-field; and as we sauntered together under the Elms, he sayth with a Sigh, "*Jack* is *Jack*, and no *More* ... he will never be anything. An' 'twere not for my beloved Wenches, I should be an unhappy Father. But what though!—My *Meg* is better unto me than ten Sons; and it maketh no Difference at Harvest-time whether our Corn were put into the Ground by a Man or a Woman."

While I was turning in my Mind what Excuse I might make for *John*, *Father* taketh me at unawares by a sudden Change of Subject; saying, "Come, tell me, *Meg*, why canst not affect *Will Roper*?"

I was a good while silent, at length made Answer, "He is so unlike alle I esteem and admire ... so unlike alle I have been taught to esteem and admire by you."—

"Have at you," he returned laughing, "I wist not I had been sharpening Weapons agaynst myself. True, he is neither *Achilles* nor *Hector*, nor even *Paris*, but yet well enough, meseems, as Times go—smarter and comelier than either *Heron* or *Dancey*."

I, faltering, made Answer, "Good Looks affect me but little—'tis in his better Part I feel the Want. He cannot ... discourse, for instance, to one's Mind and Soul, like unto you, dear *Father*, or *Erasmus*."

"I should marvel if he could," returned *Father* gravelie, "thou art mad, my Daughter, to look, in a Youth of *Will's* Years, for the Mind of a Man of fifty. What were *Erasmus* and I, dost thou suppose, at *Will's* age? Alas, *Meg*, I should not like you to know what I was! Men called me the Boy-sage, and I know not what, but in my Heart and Head was a World of Sin and Folly. Thou mightst as well expect *Will* to have my Hair, Eyes, and Teeth, alle getting the worse for Wear, as to have the Fruits of my life-long Experience, in some Cases full dearly bought. Take him for what he is, match him by the young Minds of his owne standing: consider how long and closelie we have known him. His Parts are, surelie, not amiss: he hath more Book-lore than *Dancey*, more mother Wit than *Allington*."

"But why need I to concern myself about him?" I exclaymed; "*Will* is very well in his way: why should we cross each other's Paths? I am young, I have much to learn, I love my Studdies,—why interrupt them with other and less wise Thoughts?"

"Because nothing can be wise that is not practical," returned *Father*, "and I teach my Children Philosophie to fitt them for living in the World, not above it. One may spend a Life in dreaming over *Plato*, and yet goe out of it without leaving the World a whit the better for our having made Part of it. 'Tis to little Purpose we studdy, if it onlie makes us exact Perfections in others which they may in vayn seek for in ourselves. It is not even necessary or goode for us to live entirelie with congeniall Spiritts. The vigourous tempers the inert, the passionate is evened by the cool-tempered, the prosaic balances the visionarie. Woulde thy Mother suit me better, dost thou suppose, if she coulde discuss Polemicks like *Luther* or *Melancthon*? E'en thine owne sweet Mother, *Meg*, was less affected to Studdy than thou art,—she learnt to love it for my Sake, but I made her what she was."

And, with a suddain Burste of fond Recollection, he hid his Eyes on my Shoulder, and for a Moment or soe, cried bitterlie. As for me, I shed, oh! such salt Teares!...

Aug. 17th.

Entering, o' the suddain, into *Mercy's* Chamber, I founde her all be-wept and waped, poring over an old Kirtle of Mother's she had bidden her re-line with Buckram. Coulde not make out whether she were sick of her Task, had had Words with Mother, or had some secret Inquietation of her owne; but, as she is a Girl of few Words, I found I had best leave her alone after a Caress and kind Saying or two. We alle have our Troubles.

Wednesday, 19th.

Trulie may I say soe. Here have they ta'en a Fever of some low Sorte in my House of Refuge, and *Mother*, fearing it may be the Sicknesse, will not have me goe neare it, lest I should bring it home. *Mercy*, howbeit, hath besought her soe earnestlie to let her goe and nurse the Sick, that *Mother* hath granted her Prayer, on Condition she returneth not till the Fever bates ... thus setting her Life at lower Value than our owne. Deare *Mercy*! I would fayn be her Mate.

21st.

We are alle mightie glad that *Rupert Allington* hath at lengthe zealouslie embraced the Studdy of the Law. 'Twas much to be feared at the Firste there was noe Application in him, and though we alle pitied him when *Father* first broughte him Home, a pillaged, portionlesse Client, with none other to espouse his Rightes, yet 'twas a Pitie soone allied with Contempt when we founde how emptie he was, caring for nought but Archerie and Skittles and the Popinjaye out o' the House, and Dicing and Tables within, which *Father* would on noe Excuse permitt. Soe he had to conform, ruefullie enow, and hung piteouslie on Hand for awhile. I mind me of *Bess's* saying, about *Christmasse*, "Heaven send us open Weather while *Allington* is here; I don't believe he is one that will bear shutting up." Howbeit, he seemed to incline towards *Daisy*, who is handsome enow, and cannot be hindered of Two-hundred Pounds, and soe he kept within Bounds, and when *Father* got him his Cause he was mightilie thankfulle, and woulde have left us out of Hand, but *Father* persuaded him to let his Estate recover itself, and turn the mean Time to Profitt, and, in short, soe wrought on him, that he hath now become a Student in righte earneste.

22nd.

Soe we are going to lose not only Mr. *Clement*, but Mr. *Gunnel*! How sorrie we alle are! It seemeth he hath long been debating for and agaynst the Church, and at length finds his Mind soe stronglie set towards it, as he can keep out of it noe longer. Well! we shall lose a good Master, and the Church will gayn a good Servant. *Drew* will supplie his Place, that is, according to his beste, but our worthy Welshman careth soe little for young People, and is soe abstract from the World about him, that we shall oft feel our Loss. *Father* hath promised *Gonellus* his Interest with the *Cardinall*.

I fell into Disgrace for holding Speech with *Mercy* over the Pales, but she is confident there is noe Danger; the Sick are doing well, and none of the Whole have fallen sick. She sayth *Gammer Gurney* is as tender of her as if she were her Daughter, and will let her doe noe vile or paynfull Office, soe as she hath little to doe but read and pray for the poor Souls, and feed 'em with savourie Messes, and they are alle so harmonious and full of Cheer, as to be like Birds in a Nest. *Mercy* deserves theire Blessings more than I. Were I a free Agent, she should not be alone now, and I hope ne'er to be withheld therefrom agayn.

**"I FELL INTO DISGRACE FOR HOLDING SPEECH WITH MERCY
OVER THE PALES."**
Drawn by John Jellicoe and Herbert Railton

30th.

Busied with my Flowers the chief o' the Forenoon, I was fayn to rest in the Pavilion, when, entering therein, whom shoulde I stumble upon but *William*, layd at length on the Floor, with his Arms under his Head, and his Book on the Ground. I was withdrawing brisklie enow, when he called out, "Don't goe away, since you *are* here," in a Tone soe rough, soe unlike his usuall Key, as that I paused in a Maze, and then saw that his Eyes were red. He sprung to his Feet and sayd, "*Meg*, come and talk to me;" and, taking my Hand in his, stepped quicklie forthe without another Word sayd, till we reached the Elm-tree Walk. I marvelled to see him soe moven, and expected to hear Somewhat that shoulde displease me, scarce knowing what; however, I might have guest at it from then till now, without ever nearing the Truth. His first Words were, "I wish *Erasmus* had ne'er crost the Thresholde; he has made me very unhappie;" then, seeing me stare, "Be not his Council just now, deare *Meg*, but bind up, if thou canst, the Wounds he has made.... There be some Wounds, thou knowest, though but of a cut Finger or the like, that we cannot well bind up for ourselves."

I made Answer, "I am a young and unskilled Leech."

He replyed, "But you have a quick Wit, and Patience, and Kindnesse, and for a Woman, are not scant of Learning."

"Nay," I sayd, "but Mr. *Gunnel*—"

"*Gunnel* would be the Last to help me," interrupts *Will*, "nor can I speak to your Father. He is alwaies too busie now ... besides,—"

"Father *Francis*?" I put in.

"Father *Francis*?" repeats *Will*, with a Shake o' the Head and a ruefulle Smile; "dost thou think, *Meg*, he coulde answer me if I put to him *Pilate's* Question, 'What is Truth?'"

"We know alreadie," quoth I.

Sayth *Will*, "What do we know?"

I paused, then made Answer reverentlie, "That *Jesus* is the Way, the Truth, and the Life."

"Yes," he exclaymed, clapping his Hands together in a strange Sort of Passion; "that we *doe* know, blessed be GOD, and other Foundation can or ought noe Man to lay than that is layd, which is JESUS CHRIST. But, *Meg*, is this the Principle of our Church?"

"Yea, verily," I steadfastlie replied.

"Then, how has it beene overlayd," he hurriedlie went on, "with Men's Inventions! St. *Paul* speaks of a Sacrifice once offered: we holde the Host to be a continuall Sacrifice. Holy Writ telleth us, where a Tree falls it must lie; we are taughte that our Prayers may free Souls from Purgatorie. The Word sayth, 'By Faith ye are saved;' the Church sayth, we may be saved by our Works. It is written, 'The Idols he shall utterly abolish;' we worship Figures of Gold and Silver...." "Hold, hold," I sayd, "I dare not listen to this.... You are wrong, you know you are wrong."

"How and where?" he sayth; "onlie tell me. I long to be put righte."

"Our Images are but Symbols of our Saints," I made Answer; "'tis onlie the Ignorant and Unlearned that worship the mere Wood and Stone."

"But why worship Saints at alle?" persisted *Will*; "where's your Warrant for it?"

I sayd, "Heaven has warranted it by sundrie and speciall Miracles at divers Times and Places. I may say to you, *Will*, as *Socrates* to *Agathon*, 'You may easilie argue agaynst me, but you cannot argue agaynst the Truth.'"

"Oh, put me not off with *Plato*," he impatientlie replyed, "refer me but to Holie Writ."

"How can I," quoth I, "when you have ta'en away my Testament ere I had half gone through it? 'Tis this Book, I fear me, poor *Will*, hath unsettled thee. Our Church, indeed, sayth the Unlearned wrest it to theire Destruction."

"And yet the Apostle sayth," rejoyned *Will*, "that it contayns alle Things necessarie to our Salvation."

"Doubtlesse it doth, if we knew but where to find them," I replied.

"And how find, unlesse we seeke?" he pursued, "and how know which Road to take, when we find the Scripture and the Church at Issue?"

"Get some wiser Head to advise us," I rejoyned.

"But an' if the Obstacle remains the same?"

"I cannot suppose that," I somewhat impatientlie returned, "God's Word and God's Church must agree; 'tis only we that make them at Issue."

"Ah, *Meg*, that is just such an Answer as Father *Francis* mighte give—it solves noe Difficultie. If, to alle human Reason, they pull opposite Ways, by which shall we abide? I know; I am certain. '*Tu, Domine Jesu, es Justicia mea!*'"

He looked soe rapt, with claspt Hands and upraysed Eyes, as that I coulde not but look on him and hear him with Solemnitie. At length I sayd, "If you know and are certayn, you have noe longer anie Doubts for me to lay, and with your Will, we will holde this Discourse noe longer, for however moving and however considerable its Subject Matter may be, it approaches forbidden Ground too nearlie for me to feel it safe, and I question whether it savoureth not of Heresie. However, *Will*, I most heartilie pitie you, and will pray for you."

"Do, *Meg*, do," he replyed, "and say nought to any one of this Matter."

"Indeede I shall not, for I think 'twoulde bring you if not me into Trouble; but, since thou haste soughte my Council, *Will*, receive it now and take it...."

He sayth, "What is it?"

"To read less, pray more, fast, and use such Discipline as our Church recommends, and I question not this Temptation will depart. Make a fayr Triall."

And soe, away from him, though he woulde fain have sayd more; and I have kept mine own Worde of praying for him full earnestlie, for it pitieth me to see him in such Case.

Sept. 2nd.

Poor *Will*, I never see him look grave now, nor heare him sighe, without thinking I know the Cause of his secret Discontentation. He hath, I believe, followed my Council to the Letter, for though the Men's Quarter of the House is soe far aparte from ours, it hath come rounde to me through *Barbara*, who had it from her Brother, that Mr. *Roper* hath of late lien on the Ground, and used a knotted Cord. As 'tis one of the Acts of Mercy to relieve others, when we can, from Satanic Doubts and Inquietations, I have been at some Payns to make an Abstracte of such Passages from the Fathers, and such Narratives of noted and undeniable Miracles as cannot, I think, but carry Conviction with them, and I hope they may minister to his Soul's

Comfort.

Tuesday, 4th.

Supped with my Lord *Sands*. *Mother* played Mumchance with my Lady, but *Father*, who saith he woulde rather feast a hundred poor Men than eat at one rich Man's Table, came not in till late, on Plea of Businesse. My Lord tolde him the King had visitted him not long agone, and was soe well content with his Manor as to wish it were his owne, for the singular fine Ayr and pleasant growth of Wood. In fine, wound up the Evening with Musick. My Lady hath a Pair of fine-toned Clavichords, and a Mandoline that stands five Feet high; the largest in *England*, except that of the Lady *Mary Dudley*. The Sound, indeed, is powerfull, but methinketh the Instrument ungaynlie for a Woman. Lord *Sands* sang us a new Ballad, *"The King's Hunt's up,"* which *Father* affected hugelie. I lacked Spiritt to sue my Lord for the Words, he being soe free-spoken as alwaies to dash me; howbeit, I mind they ran somewhat thus....

"The Hunt is up, the Hunt is up,
And it is well nigh Daye,
Harry our King has gone hunting
To bring his Deere to baye.
The East is bright with Morning Lighte,
And Darkness it is fled,
And the merrie Horn wakes up the Morn
To leave his idle Bed.
Beholde the Skies with golden Dyes,
Are...."

"LORD SANDS SANG US A NEW BALLAD."
Drawn by John Jellicoe

—The Rest hath escaped me, albeit I know there was some Burden of Hey-tantara, where my Lord did stamp and snap his Fingers. He is a merry Heart.

1524, October.

Sayth Lord *Rutland* to my Father, in his acute sneering Way, "Ah, ah, Sir *Thomas, Honores mutant Mores.*"

"Not so, in Faith, my Lord," returns *Father*, "but have a care lest we translate the Proverb, and say Honours change *Manners.*"

It served him right, and the Jest is worth preserving, because 'twas not premeditate, as my Lord's very likely was, but retorted at once and in Self-defence. I don't believe Honours *have* changed the *Mores*. As *Father* told *Mother*, there's the same Face under the Hood. 'Tis comique, too, the Fulfilment of *Erusmus* his Prophecy. *Plato's* Year has not come rounde, but they have got *Father* to Court, and the King seems minded never to let him goe. For us, we have the same untamed Spiritts and unconstrayned Course of Life as ever, neither lett nor hindered in our daylie Studdies, though we dress somewhat braver, and see more Companie. *Mother's* Head was a little turned, at first, by the Change and Enlargement of the Householde ... the Acquisition of Clerk of the Kitchen, Surveyor of the Dresser, Yeoman of the Pastrie, etc., but, as *Father* laughinglie tolde her, the Increase of her Cares soon steddied her Witts, for she found she had twenty Unthrifts to look after insteade of half-a-dozen. And the same with himself. His Responsibilities are soe increast, that he grutches at everie Hour the Court steals from his Family, and vows, now and then, he will leave off joking, that the King may the sooner wearie of him. But this is onlie in Jest, for he feels it is a *Power* given him over lighter Minds, which he may exert to usefull and high Purpose. Onlie it keepeth him from needing *Damocles* his Sword; he trusts not in the Favour of Princes nor in the Voyce of the People, and keeps his Soul as a weaned Child. 'Tis much for us now to get an Hour's Leisure with him, and makes us feel what our olde Privilleges were when we knew 'em not. Still, I'm pleased without being over elated, at his having risen to his proper Level.

The *King* tooke us by Surprise this Morning: *Mother* had scarce time to slip on her Scarlett Gown and Coif, ere he was in the House. His Grace was mighty pleasant to all, and, at going, saluted all round, which *Bessy* took humourously, *Daisy* immoveablie, *Mercy* humblie, I distastefullie, and *Mother* delightedlie. She calls him a fine Man; he is indeede big enough, and like to become too big; with long slits of Eyes that gaze freelie on all, as who shoulde say, "Who dare let or hinder us?" His Brow betokens Sense and Franknesse, his Eyebrows are supercilious, and his Cheeks puffy. A rolling, straddling Gait, and abrupt Speech.

T'other Evening, as *Father* and I were, unwontedly, strolling together down the Lane, there accosts us a shabby poor Fellow, with something unsettled in his Eye....

"Master, Sir Knight, and may it please your Judgeship, my name is *Patteson*."

"Very likely," says *Father*, "and my Name is *More*, but what is that to the Purpose?"

"And that is *more* to the Purpose, you mighte have said," returned the other.

"Why, soe I mighte," says *Father*, "but how shoulde I have proved it?"

"You who are a Lawyer shoulde know best about that," rejoyned the poor Knave; "'tis too hard for poor *Patteson*."

"Well, but who are you?" says *Father*, "and what do you want of me?"

"Don't you mind me?" says *Patteson*; "I played Hold-your-tongue, last *Christmasse* Revel was five Years, and they called me a smart Chap then, but last *Martinmasse* I fell from the Church Steeple, and shook my Brain-pan, I think, for its Contents have seemed addled ever since; soe what I want now is to be made a Fool."

"Then you are not one already?" says *Father*.

"If I were," says *Patteson*, "I shoulde not have come to *you*."

"Why, Like cleaves to Like, you know they say," says *Father*.

"Aye," says t'other, "but I've Reason and Feeling enow, too, to know you are no Fool, though I thoughte you might want one. Great People like 'em at their Tables, I've hearde say, though I am sure I can't guesse why, for it makes me sad to see Fools laughed at; ne'erthelesse, as I get laughed at alreadie, methinketh I may as well get paid for the Job if I can, being unable, now, to doe a Stroke of Work in hot Weather. And I'm the onlie Son of my Mother, and she is a Widow. But perhaps I'm not bad enough."

"I know not that, poor Knave," says *Father*, touched with quick Pity, "and, for those that laugh at Fools, my Opinion, *Patteson*, is that they are the greater Fools who laugh. To tell you the Truth, I had had noe Mind to take a Fool into mine Establishment, having alwaies had a Fancy to be prime Fooler in it myselfe; however, you incline me to change my Purpose, for as I said anon, Like cleaves to Like, soe, I'll tell you what we will doe—divide the Businesse and goe Halves—I continuing the Fooling, and thou receiving the Salary; that is, if I find, on Inquiry, thou art given to noe Vice, including that of Scurrillitie."

"May it like your Goodness," says poor *Patteson*, "I've been the Subject, oft, of Scurrillitie, and affect it too little to offend that Way myself. I ever keep a civil Tongue in my Head, 'specially among young Ladies."

"That minds me," says *Father*, "of a Butler who sayd he always was sober, especially when he only had Water to drink. Can you read and write?"

"Well, and what if I cannot?" returns *Patteson*, "there ne'er was but one, I ever heard of, that knew Letters, never having learnt, and well he might, for he made them that made them."

"*Meg*, there is Sense in this poor Fellow," says *Father*, "we will have him Home and be kind to him."

And, sure enow, we have done so and been so ever since.

Tuesday, 25th.

A glance at the anteceding Pages of this *Libellus* me-sheweth poor *Will Roper* at the Season his Love-fitt for me was at its Height. He troubleth me with it noe longer, nor with his religious Disquietations. Hard Studdy of the Law hath filled his Head with other Matters, and made him infinitely more rationall, and by Consequents, more agreeable. 'Twas one of those Preferences young People sometimes manifest, themselves know neither why nor wherefore, and are shamed, afterwards, to be reminded of. I'm sure I shall ne'er remind him. There was nothing in me to fix a rational or passionate Regard. I have neither *Bess's* Witt nor white Teeth, nor *Daisy's* dark Eyes, nor *Mercy's* Dimple. A plain-favoured Girl, with changefulle Spiritts,—that's alle.

26th.

Patteson's latest Jest was taking Precedence of *Father* yesterday with the Saying, "Give place, Brother; you are but Jester to King *Harry*, and I'm Jester to Sir *Thomas More*; I'll leave you to decide which is the greater Man of the two."

"Why, Gossip," cries *Father*, "his Grace woulde make two of me."

"Not a Bit of it," returns *Patteson*, "he's big enow for two such as you are, I grant ye, but the King can't make two of you. No! Lords and Commons may make a King, but a King can't make a Sir *Thomas More*."

"Yes, he can," rejoyns *Father*, "he can make me Lord Chancellor, and then he will make me more than I am already; *ergo*, he will make Sir *Thomas* more."

"But what I mean is," persists the Fool, "that the King can't make such another as you are, any more than all the King's Horses and all the King's Men can put *Humpty-dumpty* together again, which is an ancient Riddle, and full of Marrow. And soe he'll find, if ever he lifts thy Head off from thy Shoulders, which God forbid!"

Father delighteth in sparring with *Patteson* far more than in jesting with the King, whom he alwaies looks on as a Lion that may, any Minute, fall on him and rend him. Whereas, with t'other, he ungirds his Mind. Their Banter commonly exceeds not Pleasantrie, but *Patteson* is ne'er without an Answer; and although, maybe, each amuses himselfe now and then with thinking, "I'll put him up with such a Question," yet, once begun, the Skein runs off the Reel without a Knot, and shews the excellent Nature of both, soe free are they alike from Malice and Over-license. Sometimes theire Cuts are neater than common Listeners apprehend. I've seene *Rupert* and *Will*, in fencing, make theire Swords flash in the Sun at every Parry and Thrust; agayn, owing to some Change in mine owne Position, or the Decline of the Sun, the Scintillations have escaped me, though I've known their Rays must have been emitted in some Quarter alle the same.

Patteson, with one of *Argus's* cast Feathers in his Hand, is at this Moment beneath my Lattice, astride on a Stone Balustrade; while *Bessy*, whom he much affects, is sitting on the Steps, feeding her Peacocks. Sayth *Patteson*, "Canst tell me, Mistress, why Peacocks have soe manie Eyes in theire Tails, and yet can onlie see with two in theire Heads?"

"Because those two make them soe vain alreadie, Fool," says *Bess*, "that were they always beholding theire owne Glory, they woulde be intolerable."

"And besides that," says *Patteson*, "the less we see or heare, either, of what passes behind our Backs, the better for us, since Knaves will make Mouths at us then, for as glorious as we may be. Canst tell me, Mistress, why the Peacock was the last Bird that went into the Ark?"

"First tell me, Fool," returns *Bess*, "how thou knowest that it was soe?"

"Nay, a Fool may ask a Question would puzzle a Wiseard to answer," rejoyns *Patteson*; "I mighte ask you, for example, where they got theire fresh Kitchen-stuff in the Ark, or whether the Birds ate other than Grains, or the wild Beasts other than Flesh. It needs must have been a Granary."

"We ne'er shew ourselves such Fools," says *Bess*, "as in seeking to know more than is written. They had enough, if none to spare, and we scarce can tell how little is enough for bare Sustenance in a State of perfect Inaction. If the Creatures were kept low, they were all the less fierce."

"Well answered, Mistress," says *Patteson*, "but tell me, why do you wear two Crosses?"

"Nay, Fool," returns *Bess*, "I wear but one."

"Oh, but I say you wear two," says *Patteson*, "one at your Girdle, and one that nobody sees. We alle wear the unseen one, you know. Some have theirs of Gold, alle carven and shaped, soe as you hardlie tell it for a Cross ... like my Lord Cardinall, for Instance ... but it is one, for alle that. And others, of Iron, that eateth into their Hearts ... methinketh Master *Roper's* must be one of 'em. For me, I'm content with one of Wood, like that our deare LORD bore; what was goode enow for him is goode enow for me, and I've noe Temptation to shew it, as it isn't fine, nor yet to chafe at it for being rougher than my Neighbour's, nor yet to make myself a second because it is not hard enow. Doe you take me, Mistress?"

"I take you for what you are," says *Bess*, "a poor Fool."

"Nay, Niece," says *Patteson*, "my Brother your Father hath made me rich."

"I mean," says *Bess*, "you have more Wisdom than Witt, and a real Fool has neither, therefore you are only a make-believe Fool."

"Well, there are many make-believe Sages," says *Patteson*; "for mine owne Part, I never aim to be thoughte a *Hiccius Doccius*."

"A *hic est doctus*, Fool, you mean," interrupts *Bess*.

"Perhaps I do," rejoins *Patteson*, "since other Folks soe oft know better what we mean than we know ourselves. Alle I woulde say is, I ne'er set up for a Conjuror. One can see as far into a Millstone as other People, without being that. For Example, when a Man is overta'en with Qualms of Conscience for having married his Brother's Widow, when she is noe longer soe young and fair as she was a Score of Years ago, we know what that's a Sign of. And when an *Ipswich* Butcher's Son takes on him the State of my Lord *Pope*, we know what that's a Sign of. Nay, if a young Gentlewoman become dainty at her Sizes, and sluttish in her Apparel, we ... as I live, here comes *Giles Heron*, with a Fish in's Mouth."

Poor Bess involuntarilie turned her Head quicklie towards the Watergate; on which, *Patteson*, laughing as he lay on his Back, points upward with his Peacock's Feather, and cries, "Overhead, Mistress! see, there he goes. Sure, you lookt not to see Master *Heron* making towards us between the Posts and Flower-pots, eating a dried Ling?" laughing as wildly as though he were verily a Natural.

Bess, without a Word, shook the Crumbs from her Lap, and was turning into the House, when he withholds her a Minute in a perfectly altered Fashion, saying, "There be some Works, Mistress, our Confessors tell us be Works of Supereroga-tion ... is not that the Word? I learn a long one now and then ... such as be setting Food before a full Man, or singing to a deaf one, or buying for one's Pigs a Silver Trough, or, for the Matter of that, casting Pearls before a Dunghill Cock, or fishing for a Heron, which is well able to fish for itself, and is an ill-natured Bird after all, that pecks the Hand of his Mistress, and, for all her Kindness to him, will not think of *Bessy More*."

How apt alle are to abuse unlimited License! Yet 'twas good Counsel.

1525, July 2.

Soe my Fate is settled. Who knoweth at Sunrise what will chance before Sun-sett? No; the Greeks and Romans mighte speake of Chance and of Fate, but we must not. *Ruth's Hap* was to light on the Field of *Boaz*: but what she thought casual, the Lord had contrived.

Firste, he gives me the Marmot. Then, the Marmot dies. Then, I, having kept the Creature soe long, and being naturallie tender, must cry a little over it. Then *Will* must come in and find me drying mine Eyes. Then he must, most unreason-ablie, suppose that I could not have loved the poor Animal for its owne Sake soe much as for his; and, thereupon, falle a love-making in such downrighte Earneste, that I, being alreadie somewhat upset, and knowing 'twoulde please *Father* ... and hating to be perverse, ... and thinking much better of *Will* since he hath studdied soe hard, and given soe largelie to the Poor, and left off broaching his heteroclite Opinions ... I say, I supposed it must be soe, some Time or another, soe 'twas noe Use hanging back for ever and ever, soe now there's an End, and I pray God give us a quiet Life.

Noe one woulde suppose me reckoning on a quiet Life if they knew how I've cried alle this Forenoon, ever since I got quit of *Will*, by *Father's* carrying him off to *Westminster*. He'll tell *Father*, I know, as they goe along in the Barge, or else com-ing back, which will be soone now, though I've ta'en no Heed of the Hour. I wish 'twere cold Weather, and that I had a sore Throat, or stiff Neck, or somewhat that might reasonablie send me a-bed, and keep me there till to-morrow Morning. But I'm quite well, and 'tis the Dog-days, and Cook is thumping the Rolling-pin on the Dresser, and Dinner is being served, and here comes *Father*.

1528, Sept.

Father hath had some Words with the Cardinall. 'Twas touching the Draught of some forayn Treaty which the Cardinall offered for his Criticism, or rather, for his Commendation, which *Father* could not give. This nettled his Grace, who exclaimed,—"By the Mass, thou art the veriest Fool of all the Council." *Father*, smiling, rejoined, "God be thanked, that the King our Master hath but one Fool therein."

The *Cardinall* may rage, but he can't rob him of the royal Favour. The *King* was here yesterday, and walked for an Hour or soe about the Garden, with his Arm round *Father's* Neck. *Will* coulde not help felicitating *Father* upon it afterwards; to which *Father* made Answer, "I thank God I find his Grace my very good Lord indeed, and I believe he doth as singularly favour me as any Subject within this Realm. Howbeit, son *Roper*, I may tell thee between ourselves, I feel no Cause to be proud thereof, for if my Head would win him a Castle in *France*, it shoulde not fail to fly off."

"THE KING WAS HERE YESTERDAY."
Drawn by John Jellicoe and Herbert Railton

—*Father* is graver than he used to be. No Wonder. He hath much on his Mind; the Calls on his Time and Thoughts are beyond Belief; but GOD is very good to him. His Favour at home and abroad is immense: he hath good Health, soe have we alle; and his Family are established to his Mind, and settled alle about him, still under the same fostering Roof. Considering that I am the most ordinarie of his Daughters, 'tis singular I should have secured the best Husband. *Daisy* lives peaceablie with *Rupert Allington*, and is as indifferent, me seemeth, to him as to alle the World beside. He, on his Part, loves her and theire Children with Devotion, and woulde pass half his Time in the Nurserie. *Dancey* always had a hot Temper, and now and then plagues *Bess*; but she lets noe one know it but me. Sometimes she comes into my Chamber and cries a little, but the next kind Word brightens her up, and I verilie believe her Pleasures far exceed her Payns. *Giles Heron* lost her through his own Fault, and might have regained her good Opinion after all, had he taken half the Pains for her Sake he now takes for her younger Sister: I cannot think how *Cecy* can favour him; yet I suspect he will win her, sooner or later. As to mine own deare *Will*, 'tis the kindest, purest Nature, the finest Soul, the ... and yet how I was senselesse enow once to undervalue him!

Yes, I am a happy Wife; a happy Daughter; a happy Mother. When my little *Bill* stroaked dear *Father's* Face just now, and murmured "Pretty!" he burst out a-laughing, and cried,—

"You are like the young *Cyrus*, who exclaimed,—'Oh! Mother, how pretty is my Grandfather!' And yet, according to *Xenophon*, the old Gentleman was soe rouged and made up, as that none but a Child woulde have admired him!"

"That's not the Case," I observed, "with *Bill's* Grandfather."

"He's a *More* all over," says *Father*, fondly. "Make a Pun, *Meg*, if thou canst, about *Amor*, *Amore*, or *Amores*. 'Twill onlie be the thousand and first on our Name. Here, little Knave, see these Cherries: tell me who thou art, and thou shalt have one. '*More! More!*' I knew it, sweet Villain. Take them all."

I oft sitt for an Hour or more, watching *Hans Holbein* at his Brush. He hath a rare Gift of limning; and has, besides, the Advantage of deare *Erasmus* his Recommendation, for whom he hath alreddie painted our Likenesses, but I think he has made us very ugly. His Portraiture of my Grandfather is marvellous; ne'erthelesse, I look in vayn for the Spirituallitie which our *Lucchese* Friend, *Antonio Bonvisi*, tells us is to be found in the Productions of the Italian Schools.

Holbein loves to paint with the Lighte coming in upon his Work from above. He says a Lighte from above puts Objects in theire proper Lighte, and shews theire just Proportions; a Lighte from beneath reverses alle the naturall Shadows. Surelie, this hath some Truth if we spirituallize it.

June 2d.

Rupert's Cousin, *Rosamond Allington*, is our Guest. She is as beautiful as ... not as an Angel, for she lacks the Look of Goodness, but very beautiful indeed. She cometh hither from *Hever Castle*, her Account of the Affairs whereof I like not. Mistress *Anne* is not there at present; indeed, she is now always hanging about

Court, and followeth somewhat too literallie the scriptural Injunction to *Solomon's* Spouse—to forget her Father's House. The *King* likes well enow to be compared with *Solomon*, but Mistress *Anne* is not his Spouse yet, nor ever will be, I hope. Flattery and Frenchified Habitts have spoilt her, I trow.

"SHE COMETH HITHER FROM HEVER CASTLE."
Drawn by Herbert Railton

Rosamond says there is not a good Chamber in the Castle; even the Ball-room, which is on the upper Floor of alle, being narrow and low. On a rainy Day, long ago, she and Mistress *Anne* were playing at Shuttlecock therein, when *Rosamond's* Foot tripped at some Unevennesse in the Floor, and Mistress *Anne*, with a Laugh, cried out, "Mind you goe not down into the Dungeon"—then pulled up a Trap-door in the Ball-room Floor, by an iron Ring, and made *Rosamond* look down into an unknown Depth; all in the blacknesse of Darkness. 'Tis an awfulle Thing to have onlie a Step from a Ball-room to a Dungeon! I'm glad we live in a modern House; we have noe such fearsome Sights here.

Sept. 26.

How many, many Tears have I shed! Poor, imprudent *Will*.

To think of his Escape from the *Cardinall's* Fangs, and yet that he will probablie repeat the Offence! This Morning *Father* and he had a long, and, I fear me, fruitless

Debate in the Garden; on returning from which, *Father* took me aside and sayd,—

"*Meg*, I have borne a long Time with thine Husband; I have reasoned and argued with him, and still given him my poor, fatherly Counsel; but I perceive none of alle this can call him Home agayn. And therefore, *Meg*, I will no longer dispute with him." ... "Oh, *Father!*" ... "Nor yet will I give him over; but I will set another Way to work, and get me to GOD and pray for him."

And have not I done so alreadie?

27th.

I feare me they parted unfriendlie; I hearde *Father* say, "Thus much I have a Right to bind thee to, that thou indoctrinate not her in thine owne Heresies. Thou shalt not imperill the Salvation of my Child."

Since this there has been an irresistible Gloom on our Spiritts, a Cloud between my Husband's Soul and mine, without a Word spoken. I pray, but my Prayers seem dead.

Thursday, 28th.

Last Night, after seeking unto this Saint and that, methought, "Why not applie unto the Fountain Head? Maybe these holie Spiritts may have Limitations sett to the Power of theire Intercessions—at anie Rate, the Ears of *Mary-mother* are open to alle."

Soe I beganne, "*Eia mater, fons amoris.*" ...

Then methoughte, "But I am onlie asking *her* to intercede—I'll mount a Step higher still." ...

Then I turned to the greate Intercessor of alle. But methought, "Still he intercedes with another, although the same. And his owne Saying was, 'In that Day ye shall ask *me nothing*. Whatsoever ye shall ask in my Name, *he* will give it you.'" Soe I did.

I fancy I fell asleep with the Tears on my Cheek. *Will* had not come up Stairs. Then came a heavie, heavie Sleep, not such as giveth Rest; and a dark, wild Dream. Methought I was tired of waiting for *Will*, and became alarmed. The Night seemed a Month long, and at last I grew soe weary of it, that I arose, put on some Clothing, and went in search of him whom my Soul loveth. Soon I founde him, sitting in a Muse; and said, "*Will*, deare *Will?*" but he hearde me not; and, going up to touch him, I was amazed to be broughte short up or ever I reached him, by Something invisible betwixt us, hard, and cleare, and colde, ... in short, a Wall of Ice! Soe it seemed, in my strange Dreame. I pushed at it, but could not move it; called to him, but coulde not make him hear: and all the While my Breath, I suppose, raised a Vapour on the glassy Substance, that grew thicker and thicker, soe as slowlie to hide him from me. I coulde discerne his Head and Shoulders, but not see down to his Heart. Then I shut mine Eyes in Despair, and when I opened 'em, he was hidden altogether.

Then I prayed. I put my hot Brow agaynst the Ice, and I kept a weeping hot Tears, and the warm Breath of Prayer kept issuing from my Lips; and still I was persisting, when, or ever I knew how, the Ice beganne to melt! I felt it giving Way! and, looking up, coulde in joyfulle Surprize just discerne the Lineaments of a Figure close at t'other Side; the Face turned away, but yet in the Guise of listening. And, Images being apt to seem magnified and distorted through Vapours, methought 'twas altogether bigger than *Will*, yet himself, nothingthelesse; and, the Barrier between us having sunk away to Breast-height, I layd mine Hand on's Shoulder, and he turned his Head, smiling, though in Silence; and ... oh, Heaven! 'twas not *Will*, but— —.

What coulde I doe, even in my Dreame, but fall at his Feet? What coulde I doe, waking, but the same? 'Twas Grey of Morn; I was feverish and unrefreshed, but I wanted noe more lying a-bed. *Will* had arisen and gone forthe; and I, as quicklie as I coulde make myself readie, sped after him.

I know not what I expected, nor what I meant to say. The Moment I opened the Door of his Closett, I stopt short. There he stoode, in the Centre of the Chamber; his Hand resting flat on an open Book, his Head raised somewhat up, his Eyes fixed on Something or some One, as though in speaking Communion with 'em; his whole Visage lightened up and glorifide with an unspeakable Calm and Grandeur that seemed to transfigure him before me; and, when he hearde my Step, he turned about, and 'steade of histing me away, helde out his Arms.... We parted without neede to utter a Word.

June, 1530.

Events have followed too quick and thick for me to note 'em. Firste, *Father's* Embassade to *Cambray*, which I shoulde have grieved at more on our owne Accounts, had it not broken off alle further Collision with *Will*. Thoroughlie homesick, while abroad, poor *Father* was; then, on his Return, he noe sooner sett his Foot a-land, than the King summoned him to *Woodstock*. 'Twas a Couple o' Nights after he left us, that *Will* and I were roused by *Patteson's* shouting beneath our Window, "Fire, Fire, quoth *Jeremiah*!" and the House was a-fire, sure enow. Greate Part of the Men's Quarter, together with alle the Out-houses and Barns, consumed without Remedie, and alle through the Carelessnesse of *John Holt*. Howbeit, noe Lives were lost, nor any one much hurt; and we thankfullie obeyed deare *Father's* Behest, soe soone as we received the same, that we woulde get us to Church, and there, upon our Knees, return humble and harty Thanks to ALMIGHTY GOD for our late Deliverance from a fearfulle Death. Alsoe, at *Father's* Desire, we made up to the poor People on our Premises theire various Losses, which he bade us doe, even if it left him without soe much as a Spoon.

But then came an equallie unlookt-for, and more appalling Event: the Fall of my *Lord Cardinall*, whereby my Father was shortlie raised to the highest Pinnacle of professional Greatnesse; being made *Lord Chancellor*, to the Content, in some Sort, of *Wolsey* himself, who sayd he was the onlie Man fit to be his Successor.

The unheard-of Splendour of his Installation dazzled the Vulgar; while the Wisdom that marked the admirable Discharge of his daylie Duties, won the Respect of alle thinking Men, but surprized none who alreadie knew *Father*. On the Day succeeding his being sworn in, *Patteson* marched hither, and thither, bearing a huge Placard, inscribed, "Partnership Dissolved;" and apparelled himself in an old Suit, on which he had bestowed a Coating of black Paint, with Weepers of white Paper; assigning for't that "his Brother was dead." "For now," quoth he, "that they've made him *Lord Chancellor*, we shall ne'er see Sir *Thomas* more."

Now, although the poor *Cardinall* was commonlie helde to shew much Judgment in his Decisions, owing to the naturall Soundness of his Understanding, yet, being noe Lawyer, Abuses had multiplied during his Chancellorship, more especiallie in the Way of enormous Fees and Gratuities. *Father*, not content with shunning base Lucre in his proper Person, will not let anie one under him, to his Knowledge, touch a Bribe; whereat *Dancey*, after his funny Fashion, complains, saying,—

"The Fingers of my *Lord Cardinall's* veriest Door-keepers were tipt with Gold, but I, since I married your Daughter, have got noe Pickings; which in your Case may be commendable, but in mine is nothing profitable."

Father, laughing, makes Answer,—

"Your Case is hard, Son *Dancey*, but I can onlie say for your Comfort, that, soe far as Honesty and Justice are concerned, if mine owne Father, whom I reverence dearly, stoode before me on the one Hand, and the Devil, whom I hate extremely, on the other, yet, the Cause of the latter being just, I shoulde give the Devil his Due."

Giles Heron hath found this to his Cost. Presuming on his near Connexion with my Father, he refused an equitable Accommodation of a Suit, which, thereon, coming into Court, *Father's* Decision was given flat agaynst him.

His Decision agaynst *Mother* was equallie impartiall, and had Something comique in it. Thus it befelle.—A Beggar-woman's little Dog, which had beene stolen from her, was offered my *Mother* for Sale, and she bought it for a Jewel of no greate Value. After a Week or soe, the Owner finds where her Dog is, and cometh to make Complaynt of the Theft to *Father*, then sitting in his Hall. Sayth *Father*, "Let's have a faire Hearing in open Court; thou, Mistress, stand there where you be, to have impartial Justice; and thou, Dame *Alice*, come up hither, because thou art of the higher Degree. Now then, call each of you the Puppy, and see which he will follow." Soe *Sweetheart*, in spite of *Mother*, springs off to the old Beggar-woman, who, unable to keep from laughing, and yet moved at Mother's Losse, sayth,—

"Tell 'ee what, Mistress ... thee shalt have 'un for a Groat."

"Nay," sayth *Mother*, "I won't mind giving thee a Piece of Gold;" soe the Bargain was satisfactorily concluded.

THE BEGGAR-WOMAN'S DOG.
Drawn by John Jellicoe

Father's Despatch of Businesse is such, that, one Morning before the End of Term, he was tolde there was noe other Cause nor Petition to be sett before him; the which, being a Case unparalleled, he desired mighte be formally recorded.

He ne'er commences Businesse in his owne Court without first stepping into the Court of King's Bench, and there kneeling down to receive my Grandfather's Blessing. *Will* sayth 'tis worth a World to see the Unction with which the deare old Man bestows it on him.

In Rogation-week, following the Rood as usuall round the Parish, *Heron* counselled him to go a Horseback for the greater Seemlinesse, but he made Answer that 'twoulde be unseemlie indeede for the Servant to ride after his Master going afoot.

His Grace of *Norfolk*, coming yesterday to dine with him, finds him in the Church-choir, singing, with a Surplice on.

"What?" cries the *Duke*, as they walk Home together, "my *Lord Chancellor* playing the Parish-clerk? Sure, you dishonour the King and his Office."

"Nay," says *Father*, smiling, "your Grace must not deem that the King, your Master and mine, will be offended at my honouring *his* Master."

Sure, 'tis pleasant to heare *Father* taking the upper Hand of these great Folks: and to have 'em coming and going, and waiting his Pleasure, because he is the Man whom the King delighteth to honour.

True, indeed, with *Wolsey* 'twas once the same; but *Father* neede not feare the same Ruin; because he hath HIM for his Friend, whom *Wolsey* said woulde not have forsaken him had he served HIM as he served his earthly Master. 'Twas a misproud Priest; and there's the Truth on't. And *Father* is not misproud; and I don't believe we are; though proud of him we cannot fail to be.

And I know not why we may not be pleased with Prosperitie, as well as patient under Adversitie; as long as we say, "Thou, LORD, hast made our Hill soe strong." 'Tis more difficult to bear with Comelinesse, doubtlesse; and envious Folks there will be; and we know alle Things have an End, and everie Sweet hath its Sour, and everie Fountain its Fall; but ... 'tis very pleasant for all that.

IN THE GARDEN.
Drawn by Herbert Railton

Tuesday, 31st, 1532.

Who coulde have thoughte that those ripe Grapes whereof dear *Gaffer* ate soe plentifullie, should have ended his Dayes? This Event hath filled the House with Mourning. He had us all about his Bed to receive his Blessing; and 'twas piteous to see *Father* fall upon his Face, as *Joseph* on the Face of *Jacob*, and weep upon him and kiss him. Like *Jacob*, my Grandsire lived to see his duteous Son attain to the Height of earthlie Glory, his Heart unspoyled and untouched.

July, 1532.

The Days of Mourning for my Grandsire are at an end; yet *Father* still goeth heavilie. This Forenoon, looking forthe of my Lattice, I saw him walking along the River Side, his Arm cast about *Will's* Neck; and 'twas a dearer Sight to my Soul than to see the *King* walking there with his Arm around *Father's* Neck. They seemed in such earnest Converse, that I was avised to ask *Will*, afterwards, what they had been saying. He told me that, after much friendly Chat together on this and that, *Father* fell into a Muse, and presently, fetching a deep Sigh, says,—

"Would to God, Son *Roper*, on Condition three Things were well established in Christendom, I were put into a Sack, and cast presently into the *Thames*." *Will* sayth,—

"What three soe great Things can they be, *Father*, as to move you to such a Wish?"

"In Faith, *Will*," answers he, "they be these.—First, that whereas the most Part of Christian Princes be at War, they were at universal Peace. Next, that whereas the Church of Christ is at present sore afflicted with divers Errors and Heresies, it were well settled in a godly Uniformity. Last, that this Matter of the *King's* Marriage were, to the Glory of God, and the Quietness of alle Parties, brought to a good Conclusion."

Indeed, this last Matter preys on my Father's Soul. He hath even knelt to the King, to refrain from exacting Compliance with his Grace's Will concerning it; movingly reminding him, even with Tears, of his Grace's own Words to him on delivering the Great Seal, "First look unto God, and, after God, unto me." But the King is heady in this Matter; stubborn as a Mule or wild Ass's Colt, whose Mouths must be held with Bit and Bridle if they be to be governed at alle; and the King hath taken the Bit between his Teeth, and there is none dare ride him. Alle for Love of a brown Girl, with a Wen on her Throat, and an extra Finger.

July 18th.

How short a Time agone it seemeth, that in my Prosperity I sayd, "We shall never be moved; Thou, Lord, of Thy goodness hast made our Hill soe strong! ... Thou didst turn away thy Face, and I was troubled!"

28th.

Thus sayth *Plato*: of Him whom he soughte, but hardly found: "Truth is his Body, and Light his Shadow." A marvellous Saying for a Heathen.

Hear also what St. *John* sayth: "God is Light; and in him is no Darkness at all." "And the Light was the Life of Men: and the Light shineth in Darkness, and the Darkness comprehended it not."

Hear also what St. *Augustine* sayth: "They are the most uncharitable towards Error who have never experienced how hard a Matter it is to come at the Truth."

Hard, indeed. Here's *Father* agaynst *Will*, and agaynst *Erasmus*, of whom he once could not speak well enough; and now he says that if he upholds such and such Opinions his dear *Erasmus* may be the Devil's *Erasmus* for what he cares. And here's *Father* at Issue with half the learned Heads in Christendom concerning the King's Marriage. And yet, for alle that, I think *Father* is in the Right.

He taketh Matters soe to Heart that e'en his Appetite fails. Yesterday he put aside his old favourite Dish of Brewis, saying, "I know not how 'tis, good *Alice*; I've lost my Stomach, I think, for my old Relishes" ... and this, e'en with a Tear in his Eye. But 'twas not the Brewis, I know, that made it start.

Aug.

He hath resigned the Great Seal! And none of us knew of his having done soe, nor e'en of his meditating it, till after Morning Prayers to-day, when, insteade of one of his Gentlemen stepping up to my Mother in her Pew with the Words, "Madam, my Lord is gone," he cometh up to her himself, with a Smile on's Face, and sayth, low bowing as he spoke, "Madam, my Lord is gone." She takes it for one of the manie Jests whereof she misses the Point; and 'tis not till we are out of Church, in the open Air, that she fully comprehends my *Lord Chancellor* is indeed gone, and she hath onlie her Sir *Thomas More*.

"AND SAYTH, LOW BOWING AS HE SPOKE, 'MADAM, MY LORD IS GONE.'"
Drawn by John Jellicoe and Herbert Railton

A Burst of Tears was no more than was to be lookt for from poor Mother; and, in Sooth, we alle felt aggrieved and mortyfide enough; but 'twas a short Sorrow; for *Father* declared that he had cast *Pelion* and *Ossa* off his Back into the bottomless Pit; and fell into such funny Antics that we were soon as merry as ever we were in our Lives. *Patteson*, so soon as he hears it, comes leaping and skipping across the Garden, crying, "A fatted Calf! let a fatted Calf be killed, Masters and Mistresses, for this my Brother who was dead is alive again!" and falls a kissing his Hand. But poor *Patteson's* Note will soon change; for *Father's* diminished State will necessitate the Dismissal of all extra Hands; and there is manie a Servant under his Roof whom he can worse spare than the poor Fool.

In the Evening he gathers us alle about him in the Pavilion, where he throws himself into his old accustomed Seat, casts his Arm about *Mother*, and cries, "How glad must *Cincinnatus* have been to spy out his Cottage again, with *Racilia* standing at the Gate!" Then, called for Curds and Cream; sayd how sweet the soft Summer Air was coming over the River, and bade *Cecil* sing "The King's Hunt's up." After this, one Ballad after another was called for, till alle had sung their Lay, ill or well, he listing the While with closed Eyes, and a composed Smile about his Mouth; the two Furrows between his Brows relaxing graduallie till at length they could no more be seene. At last he says, —

"Who was that old Prophet that could not or would not prophesy for a King of *Judah* till a Minstrel came and played unto him? Sure, he must have loved, as I do, the very lovely Song of one that playeth well upon an Instrument, yclept the Human Heart; and have felt, as I do now, the Spirit given him to speak of Matters foreign to his Mind. 'Tis of *res angusta domi*, dear Brats, I must speak; soe, the sooner begun, the sooner over. Here am I, with a dear Wife and eight loved Children ... for my Daughters' Husbands and my Son's Wife are my Children as much as any; and *Mercy Giggs* is a Daughter too ... nine Children, then, and eleven Grandchildren, and a Swarm of Servants to boot, all of whom have as yet eaten what it pleased them, and drunken what it suited them at my Board, without its being any one's Businesse to say them nay. 'Twas the dearest Privilege of my *Lord Chancellor*; but now he's dead and gone, how shall we contract the Charges of Sir *Thomas More*?"

We looked from one to another, and were silent.

"I'll tell ye, dear ones," he went on. "I have been brought up at *Oxford*, at an Inn of Chancery, at Lincoln's Inn, and at the King's Court; from the lowest Degree, that is, to the highest; and yet have I in yearly Revenues at this Present, little above one Hundred Pounds a-year; but then, as *Chilo* sayth, 'honest Loss is preferable to dishonest Gain: by the first, a Man suffers once; by the second for ever;' and I may take up my Parable with *Samuel*, and say: 'Whose Ox have I taken? whose Ass have I taken? whom have I defrauded? whom have I oppressed? of whose Hand have I received any Bribe to blinde mine Eyes therewith?' No, my worst Enemies cannot lay to my Charge any of these Things; and my Trust in you is, that, rather than regret I should not have made a Purse by any such base Methods, you will all cheerfully contribute your Proportions to the common Fund, and share and share alike with me in this my diminished State."

We all gat about him, and by our Words and Kisses gave Warrant that we would.

"Well, then," quoth he, "my Mind is, that since we are all of a Will to walk down-hill together, we will do soe at a breathing Pace, and not drop down like a Plummet. Let all Things be done decently and in order: we won't descend to *Oxford* Fare first, nor yet to the Fare of *New Inn*. We'll begin with *Lincoln's Inn* Diet, whereon many good and wise Men thrive well; if we find this draw too heavily on the Common-Purse, we will, next Year, come down to *Oxford* Fare, with which many great and learned Doctors have been conversant; and, if our Purse stretch not to cover e'en this, why, in Heaven's Name! we'll go begging together, with Staff and Wallet, and sing a *Salve Regina* at every good Man's Door, whereby we shall still keep Company, and be merry together!"

Sept. 22d.

Now that the first Surprise and Grief, and the first Fervour of Fidelity and Self-devotion have passed off, we have subsided into how deep and holy a Quiet!

We read of the Desertion of the World, as a Matter of Course; but, when our own Turn comes, it does seem strange, to find ourselves let fall down the Stream without a single Hand outstretched to help us; forgotten, in a Moment, as though we had never been, by those who lately ate and laughed at our Table. And this, without any Fault or Offence of ours, but merely from our having lost the Light of the *King's* Countenance. I say, it does seem strange; but how fortunate, how blessed are those to whom such a Course of Events *only* seems strange, unaccompanied by Self-reproach and Bitterness! I could not help feeling this, in reading an affectionate Letter deare *Father* writ this Forenoon to *Erasmus*, wherein he sayd, "I have now obtained what, from a Child, I have continually wished! that, being entirely quit of Businesse and all publick Affairs, I might live for a Time only to God and myself."

Having no Hankering after the old Round he soe long hath run, he now, in Fact, looks younger every Day; and yet, not with the same Kind of Youth he had before his Back was bowed under the Chancellorship. 'Tis a more composed, chastised Sort of Rejuvenescence: rather the soft Warmth of Autumn, which sometimes seems like May, than May itself: the enkindling, within this mortal Tabernacle, of a heavenly Light that never grows dim, because it is immortal; and burns the same yesterday, to-day, and for ever: a Youthfulness of Soul and Mind characterised by Growth; Something with which this World and its fleeting Fancies has nothing to do: Something that the *King* can neither impart nor take away.

... We have had a tearfull Morning ... poor *Patteson* has gone. My Father hath obtained good Quarters for him with my *Lord Mayor*, with a Stipulation that he shall retain his Office with the *Lord Mayor* for the Time being, as long as he can fill it at all. This suits *Patteson*, who says he will sooner shift Masters year by year, than grow too fond of any Man again, as he hath of *Father*; but there has been sad blubbering and blowing of Noses.

Sept. 24th.

This Afternoon, coming upon *Mercy* seated in the Alcove, like unto the Image of some Saint in a Niche, her Hands folded on her Lap, and her Eyes steadfastly agaze on the setting Sun, I could not but mark how Years were silentlie at work upon her, as doubtless upon us alle; the tender, fearfulle Girl having thus graduallie changed into the sober, high-minded Woman. She is so seldom seene in Repose, so constantly astir and afoot in this or that kind Office, mostly about the Children, that I had never thought upon it before; but now I was alle at once avised to marvel that she who had so long seemed fitter for Heaven than Earth, shoulde never literallie have vowed herself the Spouse of *Christ*; more in especiall as all

Expectation of being the Spouse of anie else must long since have died within her.

I sayd, "*Mercy*, thou lookst like a Nun: how is't thou hast ne'er become one in Earnest?"

She started; then sayd, "Could I be more usefull? more harmless? less exposed to Temptation? or half so happy as I am now? In sooth, *Meg*, the Time has been when methought, how sweet the living Death of the Cloister! How good that must needs be which had the Suffrages of *Chrysostom* the golden-mouthed, and holy *Ambrose*, and our own *Anselm*! How peacefull, to take Wing like the Dove, and fly away from a naughty World, and be at Rest! How brave, to live alone, like St. *Antony*, in the Desert! only I would have had some Books with me in my Cave, and 'tis uncertayn whether St. *Antony* had Knowledge of Letters, beyond the heaven-taught Lesson, 'GOD is Love,' ... for methought so much Reflection and no Action would be too much for a Woman's Mind to bear—I might goe mad: and I remembered me how the Dove that gladly flew away from the Ark, gladly flew back, and abode in the Ark till such Time as a new Home was ready for her. And methought, cannot I live apart from Sin here, and now; and as to Sorrow, where can we live apart from that? Sure, we may live on the Skirts of the World in a Spiritt as truly unworldlie, as though we were altogether out of it: and here I may come and go, and range in the fresh Air, and love other Folks' Children, and read my Psalter, and pore over the Sayings of the wise Men of old, and look on the Faces I love, and sit at the Feet of Sir *Thomas More*. Soe there, *Meg*, are my poor Reasons for not caring to be a Nun. Our deare Lord is in himself all that our highest, holiest Affections can seek or comprehend; for he made these our Hearts; he gave us these our Affections; and through them the Spirit speaks. Aspiring to their Source, they rise up like the white Smoke and bright Flame; while, on Earth, if left unmastered, they burn, suffocate, and destroy. Yet they have their natural and innocent Outlets even here; and a Woman may warm herself by them without Scorching, and yet be neither a Wife nor a Nun."

Sept. 28th.

Ever since *Father's* Speech to us in the Pavilion, we have beene of one Heart and one Soul; neither have any of us said that aught of the Things we possessed were our own, but we have had all Things in Common. And we have eaten our Meat with Gladness and Singleness of Heart.

This Afternoon, expressing to *Father* my gratefull Sense of our present Happiness ... "Yes, *Meg*," returns he, "I too, am deeply thankful for this breathing Space."

"Do you look on it as no more, then?" I sayd.

"As no more, *Meg*: we shall have a Thunder-clap by-and-by. Look out on the *Thames*. See how unwontedlie clear it is, and how low the Swallows fly.... How distinctlie we see the green Sedges on *Battersea* Bank, and their reflected Images in the Water. We can almost discern the Features of those poor Knaves digging in the Cabbage Gardens, and hear 'em talk, so still is the Air. Have you ne'er before noted these Signs?"

"A Storm is brewing," I sayd.

"Aye, we shall have a Lightning-flash anon. So still, *Meg*, is also our moral Atmosphere just now. GOD is giving us a breathing Space, as he did to the Egyptians before the Plague of Hail, that they might gather their live Stock within Doors. Let us take for Example them that believed and obeyed him; and improve this holy Pause."

Just at this Moment, a few heavie Drops fell agaynst the Window Pane, and were seene by both. Our Eyes met; and I felt a silent Pang.

"Five Days before the *Passover*," resumed *Father*, "all seemed as still and quiet as we are now; but JESUS knew his Hour was at hand. E'en while he yet spake familiarly among the People, there came a Sound from Heaven, and they that stood by said it thundered; but *he* knew it for the Voice of his dear Father. Let us, in like Manner, when the Clap cometh, recognise in it the Voice of GOD, and not be afraid with any Amazement."

Nov. 2d.

Gammer Gurney is dead, and I must say I am glad of it. The Change, to her, must be blessed, and there seemed some Danger lest, after having escaped being ducked for a Witch, she shoulde have been burnt for a Heretic. *Father* looked on her as an obstinate old Woman; *Will* counted her little short of a Saint and Prophetess, and kept her well supplied with alle she could need. Latterly she was stone deaf; so 'tis a happy Release.

The settled Purpose of *Father's* Soul, just now, is to make up a Marriage between *Mercy* and Dr. *Clement*. 'Tis high Advancement for her, and there seems to have been some old Liking between 'em we never knew of.

1533, April 1.

Though some Months have passed since my Father uttered his warning Voice, and all continues to go quiet, I cannot forbear, now and then, to call his Monition to Mind, and look about for the Cloud that is to bring the Thunder-clap; but the Expectation sobers rather than saddens me.

This Morning, leaning over the River Wall, I was startled by the cold, damp Hand of some one from behind being laid on mine. At the same Time a familiar Voice exclaimed, "Canst tell us, Mistress, why Fools have hot Heads and Hands icy cold?"

I made Answer, "Canst tell me, *Patteson*, why Fools should stray out of Bounds?"

"Why, that's what Fools do every Day," he readily replied; "but this is *All Fools' Day*, mine own special Holiday; and I told my *Lord Mayor* overnight, that if he lookt for a Fool this Morning, he must look in the Glass. In sooth, Mistress *Meg*, I should by Rights wear the Gold Chain and he the Motley; for a proper Fool he is, and I shall be glad when his Year's Service to me is out. The worst o' these Lord Mayors is, that we can't part with 'em till their Time's up. Why now, this present one hath not so much Understanding as would foot an old Stocking; 'twas but yesterday when, in Quality of my Taster, he civilly enough makes over to me a half-eaten Plate of Gurnet, which I wave aside, thus, saying, I eat no Fish of which

I cannot affirm, '*rari sunt Boni*,' few are the Bones ... and I protest to you he knew it not for Fool's Latin. Thus I'm driven, from mere Discouragement, to leave prating for listening, which thou knowest, Mistress, is no Fool's Office; and among the sundrie Matters I hear at my Lord's Table ... for he minds not what he says before his Servants, thereby giving new Proof 'tis he shoulde wear the Motley ... I note his saying that the *King's* private Marriage will assuredlie be made publick this coming Easter, and my Lady *Anne* will be crowned ... more by token, he knows the Merchant that will supply the *Genoa* Velvet and Cloth of Gold, and the Masquers that are to enact the Pageant. For the Love o' Safety, then, Mistress *Meg*, bid thy good *Father* e'en take a Fool's Advice, and eat humble Pie betimes, for doubt not this proud Madam to be as vindictive as *Herodias*, and one that, unless he appease her full early, will have his Head set before her in a Charger. I've said my Say."

April 4th.

Three Bishops have been here this Forenoon, to bid *Father* to the Coronation, and offer him twenty Pounds to provide his Dress; but *Father* hath, with Courtesie, declined to be present. After much friendly pressing, they parted, seemingly on good Terms; but I have Misgivings of the Issue.

April 9th.

A ridiculous Charge hath beene got up 'gainst dear *Father*; no less than of Bribery and Corruption. One *Parnell* complaineth of a Decree given agaynst him in favour of one *Vaughan*, whose Wife, he deponeth, gave *Father* a gilt Flaggon. To the noe small Surprise of the Council, *Father* admitted that she had done soe: "But, my Lords," proceeded he, when they had uttered a few Sentences of Reprehension somewhat too exultantlie, "will ye list the Conclusion of the Tale? I bade my Butler fill the Cup with Wine, and having drunk her Health, I made her pledge me, and then restored her Gift, and would not take it again."

As innocent a Matter, touching the offering him a Pair of Gloves containing Forty Pounds, and his taking the first and returning the last, saying he preferred his Gloves without Lining, hath been made publick with like Triumph to his own good Fame; but alack! these Feathers show which way sets the Wind.

April 13th.

A heavier Charge than either of the above hath been got up, concerning the wicked Woman of *Kent*, with whom they accuse him of having tampered, that, in her pretended Revelations and Rhapsodies, she might utter Words against the *King's* Divorce. His Name hath, indeed, been put in the Bill of Attainder; but, out of Favour, he hath been granted a private Hearing, his Judges being, the new Archbishop, the new Chancellor, his Grace of *Norfolk*, and Master *Cromwell*.

He tells us that they stuck not to the Matter in Hand, but began cunningly enow to sound him on the *King's* Matters; and finding they could not shake him, did proceed to Threats, which, he told 'em, might well enow scare Children, but not him; and as to his having provoked his Grace the *King* to sett forth in his Book aught to dishonour and fetter a good Christian, his Grace himself well knew the Book was never shewn him save for verbal Criticism when the Subject-matter was completed *by the Makers of the same*, and that he had warned his Grace not to express soe much Submission to the Pope. Whereupon they with great Displeasure dismissed him, and he took Boat for *Chelsea* with mine Husband in such gay Spiritts, that *Will*, not having been privy to what had passed, concluded his Name to have beene struck out of the Bill of Attainder, and congratulated him thereupon soe soone as they came aland, saying, "I guess, *Father*, all is well, seeing you thus merry."

"It is, indeed, son *Roper*," returns *Father* steadilie; repeating thereupon, once or twice, this Phrase, "All is well."

Will, somehow mistrusting him, puts the Matter to him agayn.

"You are then, *Father*, put out of the Bill?"

"Out of the Bill, good Fellow?" repeats *Father*, stopping short in his Walk, and regarding him with a Smile that *Will* sayth was like to break his Heart.... "Wouldst thou know, dear Son, why I am so joyful? In good Faith, I have given the Devil a foul Fall; for I have with those Lords gone so far, as that without great Shame I can ne'er go back. The first Step, *Will*, is the worst, and that's taken."

And so, to the House, with never another Word, *Will* being smote at the Heart.

But, this Forenoon, deare *Will* comes running in to me, with Joy all bright, and tells me he hath just heard from *Cromwell* that *Father's* Name is in sooth struck out. Thereupon, we go together to him with the News. He taketh it thankfully, yet composedly, saying, as he lays his Hand on my Shoulder, "In faith, *Meg, quod differtur non aufertur*." Seeing me somewhat stricken and overborne, he sayth, "Come, let's leave good *Will* awhile to the Company of his own select and profitable Thoughts, and take a Turn together by the Water Side."

Then closing his Book, which I marked was *Plato's Phædon*, he steps forthe with me into the Garden, leaning on my Shoulder, and pretty heavilie too. After a Turn or two in Silence, he lightens his Pressure, and in a bland, peaceifying Tone commences *Horace* his tenth Ode, Book second, and goes through the first fourteen or fifteen Lines in a kind of lulling Monotone; then takes another Turn or two, ever looking at the *Thames*; and in a stronger Voice begins his favourite

> *"Justum, ac tenacem Propositi Virum*
> *Non Civium Ardor,"* etc.

on to

> *"Impavidum ferient Ruinæ;"*

—and lets go his Hold on me to extend his Hand in fine, free Action. Then, drawing me to him agayn, presentlie murmurs, "I reckon that the Sufferings of this present Time are not worthy to be compared with the Glory which shall be revealed in us.... Oh no, not worthy to be compared. I have lived; I have laboured; I have loved. I have lived in them I loved; laboured for them I loved; loved them for whom I laboured; my Labour has not been in vayn. To love and to labour is the Sum of living, and yet how manie think they live who neither labour nor love! Agayn, how manie labour and love, and yet are not loved; but I have beene loved, and my Labour has not been in vayn. Now, the Daye is far spent, and the Night is at hand, and the Time draweth nigh when Man resteth from his Labours, even from his Labours of Love; but still he shall love and he shall live where the Spiritt sayth he shall rest from his Labours, and where his Works do follow him, for he entereth into Rest through and to Him who is Life, and Light, and Love."

Then looking steadfastlie at the *Thames*, "How quietlie," sayth he, "it flows on! This River, *Meg*, hath its Origin from seven petty Springs somewhither amongst the *Gloucestershire* Hills, where they bubble forthe unnoted save by the Herd and Hind. Belike, they murmur over the Pebbles prettily enough; but a great River, mark you, never murmurs. It murmured and babbled too, 'tis like, whilst only a Brook, and brawled away as it widened and deepened and chafed agaynst Obstacles, and here and there got a Fall, and splashed and made much Ado, but ever kept running on towards its End, still deepening and widening; and now towards the Close of its Course look you how swift and quiet it is, running mostly between Flats, and with the dear blue Heaven reflected in its Face." ...

1534, April 12.

'Twas o' *Wednesdaye* was a Week, we were quietly taking our Dinner, when, after a loud and violent Knocking at the outer Door, in cometh a Pursuivant, and summoneth *Father* to appear next Daye before the Commissioners, to take the newly-coined Oath of Supremacy. *Mother* utters a hasty Cry, *Bess* turns white as Death, but I, urged by I know not what suddain Impulse to con the new Comer's Visage narrowly, did with Eagerness exclaim, "Here's some Jest of *Father's*; 'tis only *Dick Halliwell!*"

"IN COMETH A PURSUIVANT."
Drawn by John Jellicoe

Whereupon, *Father* burst out a-laughing, hugged *Mother*, called *Bess* a silly Puss, and gave *Halliwell* a Groat for's Payns. Now, while some were laughing, and others taking *Father* prettie sharplie to Task for soe rough a Crank, I fell a muzing, what could be the Drift of this, and coulde only surmize it mighte be to harden us beforehand, as 'twere, to what was sure to come at last. And the Pre-apprehension of this soe belaboured my alreadie o'erburthened Spiritts, as that I was fayn to be-take myself to the Nurserie, and lose all Thought and Reflection in my little *Bess's* prettie Ways. And, this not answering, was forct to have Recourse to Prayer; then, leaving my Closett, was able to return to the Nurserie, and forget myselfe awhile in the Mirth of the Infants.

Hearing Voyces beneathe the Lattice, I lookt forthe, and behelde his Grace of *Norfolk* (of late a strange Guest) walking beneath the Window in earnest Converse with *Father*; and, as they turned about, I hearde him say, "By the Mass, Master *More*, 'tis perilous striving with Princes. I could wish you, as a Friend, to incline to the *King's* Pleasure; for *Indignatio Principis Mors est.*"

"Is that all?" says *Father*; "why then there will be onlie this Difference between your Grace and me, that I shall die to-daye, and you to-morrow;"—which was the Sum of what I caught.

Next Morning, we were breaking our Fast with Peacefullnesse of Heart, on the Principle that sufficient for the Daye is the Evill thereof, and there had beene a wordy War between our two Factions of the *Neri* and *Bianchi*, *Bess* having defalked from the Mancheteers on the Ground that black Bread sweetened the Breath and settled the Teeth, to the no small Triumph of the Cob Loaf Party; while *Daisy*, persevering at her Crusts, sayd, "No, I can cleave to the Rye Bread as steddilie as anie among you, but 'tis vayn of *Father* to maintain that it is as toothsome as a Manchet, or that I eat it to whiten my Teeth, for thereby he robs Self-deniall of its Grace."

Father, strange to say, seemed taken at Vantage, and was pausing for a Retort, when *Hobson* coming in and whispering Somewhat in his Ear, he rose suddainlie and went forthe of the Hall with him, putting his Head back agayn to say, "Rest ye alle awhile where ye be," which we did, uneasilie enow. Anon he returns, brushing his Cap, and says calmlie, "Now, let's forthe to Church," and clips *Mother's* Arm beneathe his owne and leads the Way. We follow as soon as we can; and I, listing to him more than to the Priest, did think I never hearde him make Response more composedlie, nor sing more lustilie, by the which I founde myself in stouter Heart. After Prayers, he is shriven, after which he saunters back with us to the House; then brisklie turning on his Heel, cries to my Husband, "Now, *Will*, let's toward, Lad," and claps the Wicket after him, leaving us at t'other Side without so much as casting back a parting Look. Though he evermore had beene avised to let us companie him to the Boat, and there kiss him once and agayn or ever he went, I know not that I should have thoughte much of this, had not *Daisy*, looking after him keenly, exclaymed somewhat shortlie as she turned in Doors, "I wish I had not uttered that Quip about the Cob-loaf."

Oh, how heavilie sped the Day! The House, too big now for its Master's diminished Retinue, had yet never hitherto seemed lonesome; but now a Somewhat of drearie and dreadfull, inexpressible in Words, invisible to the Eye, but apprehended by the inner Sense, filled the blank Space alle about. For the first Time, everie one seemed idle; not only disinclined for Businesse, but as though there were Something unseemlie in addressing one's Self to it. There was nothing to cry about, nothing to talk over, and yet we alle stoode agaze at each other in Groups, like the Cattle under the Trees when a Storm is at hand. *Mercy* was the first to start off. I held her back and said, "What is to do?" She whispered, "Pray." I let her Arm drop, but *Bess* at that Instant comes up with Cheeks as colourless as Parchment. She sayth, "'Tis made out now. A Pursuivant *de Facto* fetched him forthe this Morning." We gave one deep, universal Sigh; *Mercy* broke away, and I after her, to seek the same Remedy, but alack, in vayn....

15th.

How large a Debt we owe you, wise and holie Men of old! How ye counsel us to Patience, incite us to Self-mastery, cheer us on to high Emprize, temper in us the

Heat of Youth, school our Inexperience, calm the o'erwrought Mind, allay the Anguish of Disappointment, cheat Suspense, and master Despair.... How much better and happier ye would make us, if we would but list your Teaching!

Bess hath fallen Sick; no marvell. Everie one goeth heavilie. Alle Joy is darkened; the Mirthe of the House is gone.

Will tells me, that as they pushed off from the Stairs, *Father* took him about the Neck and whispered, "I thank our Lord, the Field is won!" Sure, *Regulus* ne'er went forthe with higher Self-devotion.

THE STAIRS.
Drawn by Herbert Railton

Having declared his Inabilitie to take the Oath as it stoode, they bade him, *Will* tells me, take a Turn in the Garden while they administered it to sundrie others, thus affording him Leisure for Re-consideration. But they might as well have bidden the Neap-tide turn before its Hour. When called in agayn, he was as firm as ever, so was given in Ward to the *Abbot* of *Westminster* till the *King's* Grace was informed of the Matter. And now, the Fool's wise Saying of vindictive *Herodias* came true, for 'twas the *King's* Mind to have Mercy on his old Servant, and tender him a qualifyed Oath; but Queen *Anne*, by her importunate Clamours, did over-rule his proper Will, and at four Days' End, the full Oath being agayn tendered and rejected, *Father* was committed to the Tower. Oh, wicked Woman, how could you?... Sure, you never loved a Father....

May 22d.

In Answer to our incessant Applications throughout this last Month past, *Mother* hath at length obtayned Access to dear *Father*. She returned, her Eyes nigh swollen to closing with weeping.... We crowded round about, burning for her Report, but 'twas some Time ere she coulde fetch Breath or Heart to give it us. At length *Daisy*, kissing her Hand once and agayn, draws forthe a disjoynted Tale, somewhat after this Fashion.

"Come, give over weeping, dearest *Mother*, 'twill do neither him, you, nor us anie Goode.... What was your first Speech of him?"

"Oh, my first Speech, Sweetheart, was, 'What, my Goodness, Mr. *More*! I marvell how that you, who were always counted a wise Man, should now soe play the Fool as to lie here in this close, filthy Prison, shut up with Mice and Rats, when you mighte be abroade and at your Liberty, with the Favour of King and Council, and return to your righte fayr House, your Books and Gallery, and your Wife, Children, and Household, if soe be you onlie woulde but do what the Bishops and best learned of the Realm have, without Scruple, done alreadie.'"

"And what sayd he, *Mother*, to that?" ...

"Why, then, Sweetheart, he chucks me under the Chin and sayeth, 'I prithee, good Mistress *Alice*, to tell me one Thing.' ... Soe then I say, 'What Thing?' Soe then he sayeth, 'Is not this House, Sweetheart, as nigh Heaven as mine own?' Soe then I jerk my Head away and say, 'Tilly-valley! Tilly-valley!'"

Sayth *Bess*, "Sure, *Mother*, that was cold Comfort.... And what next?"

"Why, then I said, '*Bone Deus*, Man! *Bone Deus!* will this Gear never be left?' So then he sayth, 'Well then, Mrs. *Alice*, if it be soe, 'tis mighty well, but, for my Part, I see no greate Reason why I shoulde much joy in my gay House, or in Aniething belonging thereunto, when, if I shoulde be but seven Years buried underground, and then arise and come thither agayn, I shoulde not fail to find Some therein that woulde bid me get out of Doors, and tell me 'twas none o' mine. What Cause have I, then, to care soe greatlie for a House that woulde soe soone forget its Master?'"

"And then, *Mother*? and then?"

"Soe then, Sweetheart, he sayth, 'Come tell me, Mrs. *Alice*, how long do you think we might reckon on living to enjoy it?' Soe I say, 'Some twenty Years, forsooth.' 'In faith,' says he, 'had you said some thousand Years, it had beene Somewhat; and yet he were a very bad Merchant that woulde put himselfe in Danger to lose Eternity for a thousand Years ... how much the rather if we are not sure to enjoy it one Day to an End?' Soe then he puts me off with Questions, How is *Will*? and *Daisy*? and *Rupert*? and this one? and t'other one? and the Peacocks? and Rabbits? and have we elected a new King of the Cob-loaf yet? and has *Tom* found his Hoop? and is the Hasp of the Buttery-hatch mended yet? and how goes the Court? and what was the Text o' *Sunday*? and have I practised the Viol? and how are we off for Money? and why can't he see *Meg*? Then he asks for this Book and t'other Book, but I've forgot their Names, and he sayth he's kept mighty short of Meat, though 'tis little he eats, but his Man *John a Wood* is gay an' hungry, and 'tis worth a World to see him at a salt Herring. Then he gives me Counsell of this and that, and puts his Arm about me and says, 'Come, let us pray;' but while he kept praying for one and t'other, I kept a-counting of his gray Hairs; he'd none a Month agone. And we're scarce off our Knees, when I'm fetched away; and I say, 'When will you change your Note, and act like a wise Man?' and he sayth, 'When? when?' looking very profound; 'why, ... when Gorse is out of Blossom and Kissing out of Fashion.' Soe puts me forthe by the Shoulders with a Laugh, calling after me, 'Remember me over and over agayn to them alle, and let me see *Meg*.'"

... I feel as if a String were tied tight about my Heart. Methinketh 'twill burst if we goe on long soe.

July 25th.

He hath writ us a few Lines with a Coal, ending with "*Sursum Corda*, dear Children! up with your Hearts." The Bearer was dear *Bonvisi*.

Aug. 16th.

The Lord begins to cut us short. We are now on very meagre Commons, dear *Mother* being obliged to pay fifteen Shillings a week for the Board, poor as it is, of *Father* and his Servant. She hath parted with her Velvet Gown, embroidered over-thwart, to my Lady *Sands'* Woman. Her Mantle edged with Coney went long ago.

But we lose not Heart; I think mine is becoming annealed in the Furnace, and will not now break. I have writ somewhat after this Fashion to him.... "What do you think, most dear *Father*, doth comfort us at *Chelsea*, during this your Absence? Surelie, the Remembrance of your Manner of Life among us, your holy Conversa-tion, your wholesome Counsells, your Examples of Virtue, of which there is Hope that they do not onlie persevere with you, but that, by God's Grace, they are much increast."

I weary to see him.... Yes, we shall meet in Heaven, but how long first, O Lord? how long?

Aug 20th.

Now that I've come back, let me seek to think, to remember.... Sure, my Head will clear by-and-by! Strange, that Feeling shoulde have the Masterdom of Thought and Memory, in Matters it is most concerned to retayn.

... I minded to put the Haircloth and Cord under my Farthingale, and one or two of the smaller Books in my Pouch, as alsoe some Sweets and Suckets such as he was used to love. *Will* and *Bonvisi* were a-waiting for me; and deare *Bess*, putting forthe her Head from her Chamber Door, cries piteously, "Tell him, dear *Meg*, tell him ... 'twas never soe sad to me to be sick ... and that I hope ... I pray ... the Time may come ..." then falls back swooning into *Dancey's* Arms, whom I leave crying heartilie over her, and hasten below to receive the confused Medley of Messages sent by every other Member of the House. For mine owne Part, I was in such a tremulous Succussion as to be scarce fitt to stand or goe; but Time and the Tide will noe Man bide, and, once having taken Boat, the cool River Air allayed my fevered Spiritts; onlie I coulde not for awhile get ridd of the Impression of poor *Dancey* crying over *Bess* in her Deliquium.

I think none o' the three opened our Lips before we reached *Lambeth*, save, in the *Reach*, *Will* cried to the Steersman, "Look you run us not aground," in a sharper Voyce than I e'er heard from him. After passing the *Archbishop's* Palace, whereon I gazed full ruefullie, good *Bonvisi* beganne to mention some Rhymes he had founde writ with a Diamond on one of the Window-panes at *Crosby House*, and would know were they *Father's*? and was't the Chamber *Father* had used to sleep in? I tolde him it was, but knew Nought of the Distich, though 'twas like enow to be his. And thence he went on to this and that, how that *Father's* cheerfulle, funny Humour never forsook him, nor his brave Heart never quelled; instancing his fear-lesse Passage through the Traitor's Gate, asking his Neighbours whether *his* Gait were that of a Traditor; and, on being sued by the Porter for his upper Garment, giving him his *Cap*, which he sayd was uppermost. And other such Quips and Passages, which I scarce noted nor smiled at, soe sorry was I of Cheer.

"HIS FEARLESSE PASSAGE THROUGH THE TRAITOR'S GATE."
Drawn by John Jellicoe and Herbert Railton

At length we stayed rowing: *Will* lifted me out, kissed me, heartened me up; and, indeede, I was in better Heart then, having been quietlie in Prayer a good While. After some few Forms, we were led through sundrie Turns and Passages; and, or ever I was aware, I founde myself quit of my Companions and in *Father's*

Arms.

We both cried a little at first; I wonder I wept noe more, but Strength was given me in that Hour. As soone as I coulde, I lookt him in the Face, and he lookt at me, and I was beginning to note his hollow Cheeks, when he sayd, "Why, *Meg*, you are getting freckled;" soe that made us bothe laugh. He sayd, "You shoulde get some Freckle-water of the Lady that sent me here; depend on it, she hath Washes and Tinctures in Plenty; and after all, *Meg*, she'll come to the same End at last, and be as the Lady all Bone and Skin, whose ghastlie Legend used to scare thee soe when thou wert a Child. Don't tell that Story to thy Children; 'twill hamper 'em with unsavoury Images of Death. Tell them of heavenlie Hosts a-waiting to carry off good Men's Souls in fire-bright Chariots, with Horses of the Sun, to a Land where they shall never more be surbated and weary, but walk on cool, springy Turf and among Myrtle Trees, and eat Fruits that shall heal while they delight them, and drink the coldest of cold Water, fresh from the River of Life, and have Space to stretch themselves, and bathe, and leap, and run, and, whichever Way they look, meet *Christ's* Eyes smiling on them. Sure, *Meg*, who would live, that coulde die? One mighte as lief be an Angel shut up in a Nutshell as bide here. Fancy how gladsome the sweet Spirit woulde be to have the Shell cracked! no matter by whom; the King, or King's Mistress.... Let her dainty Foot but set him free, he'd say, 'For this Release, much Thanks.' ... And how goes the Court, *Meg*?"

"In Faith, *Father*, never better.... There is Nothing else there, I hear, but Dancing and Disporting."

"Never better, Child, sayst thou? Alas, *Meg*, it pitieth me to consider what Misery, poor Soul, she will shortlie come to. These Dances of hers will prove such Dances that she will spurn our Heads off like Footballs; but 'twill not be long ere her Head will dance the like Dance. Mark you, *Meg*, a Man that restraineth not his Passions, hath always Something cruel in his Nature, and if there be a Woman toward, she is sure to suffer heaviest for it, first or last.... Seek Scripture Precedent for't ... you'll find it as I say. Stony as Death, cruel as the Grave. Those *Pharisees* that were, to a Man, convicted of Sin, yet haled a sinning Woman before the LORD, and woulde fain have seene the Dogs lick up her Blood. When they lick up mine, deare *Meg*, let not your Heart be troubled, even though they shoulde hale thee to *London Bridge*, to see my Head stuck on a Pole. Think, most dear'st, I shall then have more Reason to weep for thee than thou for me. But there's noe weeping in Heaven; and bear in Mind, *Meg*, distinctlie, that if they send me thither, 'twill be for obeying the Law of GOD rather than of Men. And after alle, we live not in the bloody, barbarous old Times of Crucifyings and Flayings, and immersing in Cauldrons of boiling Oil. One Stroke, and the Affair's done. A clumsy Chirurgeon would be longer extracting a Tooth. We have oft agreed that the little Birds struck down by the Kite and Hawk suffer less than if they were reserved to a naturall Death. There is one sensible Difference, indeed, between us. In our Cases, Preparation is a-wanting."

Hereon, I minded me to slip off the Haircloth and Rope, and give the same to him, along with the Books and Suckets, all which he hid away privatelie, making merry at the last.

"'Twoulde tell well before the Council," quoth he, "that on searching the Prison-cell of Sir *Thomas More*, there was founde, flagitiouslie and mysteriouslie laid up … a piece of Barley-sugar!"

Then we talked over sundrie Home-matters; and anon, having now both of us attayned unto an equable and chastened Serenitie of Mind, which needed not any false Shows of Mirth to hide the naturall Complexion of, he sayth, "I believe, *Meg*, they that have put me here ween they have done me a high Displeasure; but I assure thee on my Faith, mine owne good Daughter, that if it had not beene for my Wife, and for you, my dear good Children, I woulde faine have beene closed up, long ere this, in as strait a Room, and straiter too."

Thereon, he shewed me how illegal was his Imprisonment, there being noe Statute to authorize the Imposition of the Oath, and he delivered himself, with some Displeasure, agaynst the King's ill Counsellors.

"And surelie, *Meg*," quoth he, "'tis pitie that anie Christian Prince shoulde, by a flexible Council readie to follow his Affections, and by a weak Clergy lacking Grace to stand constantly to the Truth as they have learned it, be with Flattery so constantly abused. The Lotus Fruit fabled by the Ancients, which made them that ate it lose all Relish for the daylie Bread of their own Homes, was Flattery, *Meg*, as I take it, and Nothing else. And what less was the Song of the Syrens, agaynst which *Ulysses* made his Sailors stop their Ears, and which he, with all his Wisdom, coulde not listen to without struggling to be unbound from the Mast? Even Praise, *Meg*, which, moderately given, may animate and cheer forward the noblest Minds, yet too lavishly bestowed, will decrease and palsy their Strength, e'en as an Over-dose of the most generous and sprightlie Medicine may prove mortiferous. But Flattery is noe Medicine, but a rank Poison, which hath slayn Kings, yea, and mighty Kings; and they who love it, the LORD knoweth afar off; knoweth distantlie, has no care to know intimatelie, for they are none of his."

Thus we went on, from one Theme to another, till methinketh a heavenlie Light seemed to shine alle about us, like as when the Angel entered the Prison of *Peter*. I hung upon everie Word and Thought that issued from his Lips, and drank them in as thirsty Land sucks up the tender Rain…. Had the Angel of Death at that Hour come in to fetch both of us away, I woulde not have sayd him nay, I was soe passively, soe intenselie happy. At length, as Time wore on, and I knew I shoulde soone be fetcht forthe, I coulde not but wish I had the Clew to some secret Passage or Subterraneal, of the which there were doubtless Plenty in the thick Walls, whereby we might steal off together. *Father* made Answer, "Wishes never filled a Sack. I make it my Businesse, *Meg*, to wish as little as I can, except that I were better and wiser. You fancy these four Walls lonesome; how oft, dost thou suppose, I here receive *Plato* and *Socrates*, and this and that holy Saint and Martyr? My Gaolers can noe more keep them out than they can exclude the Sunbeams. Thou knowest, JESUS stood among his Disciples when the Doors were shut. I am not more lonely than St. *Anthony* in his Cave, and I have a divine Light e'en here, whereby to con the Lesson, 'GOD is Love.' The Futility of our Enemies' Efforts to make us miserable was never more stronglie proven to me than when I was a mere Boy in *Cardinall Morton's* Service. Having unwittinglie angered one of his Chaplains, a choleric and even malignant-spirited Man, he did, of his owne Authoritie, shut me up for some Hours in a certayn damp Vault, which, to a Lad afeard of Ghosts and devilish Apparitions, would have beene fearsome enow. Howbeit, I there cast myself on the Ground with my Back sett agaynst the Wall, and mine Arm behind my Head, this Fashion ... and did then and there, by reason of a young Heart, quiet Conscience, and quick Phansy, conjure up such a lively Picture of the Queen o' the Fairies' Court, and alle the Sayings and Doings therein, that never was I more sorry than when my Gaoler let me goe free, and bade me rise up and be doing. In place, therefore, my Daughter, of thinking of me in thy Night Watches as beating my Wings agaynst my Cage Bars, trust that GOD comes to look in upon me without Knocking or Bell-ringing. Often in Spiritt I am with you alle; in the Chapel, in the Hall, in the Garden; now in the Hayfield, with my Head on thy Lap, now on the River, with *Will* and *Rupert* at the Oar. You see me not about your Path, you won't see my disembodied Spiritt beside you hereafter, but it may be close upon you once and agayn for alle that: maybe, at Times when you have prayed with most Passion, or suffered with most Patience, or performed my Hests with most Exactness, or remembered my Care of you with most Affection. And now, good Speed, good *Meg*, I hear the Key turn in the Door.... This Kiss for thy Mother, this for *Bess*, this for *Cecil*, ... this and this for my whole School. Keep dry Eyes and a hopefull Heart; and reflect that Nought but unpardoned Sin shoulde make us weep for ever."

September.

Seeing the Woodman fell a noble Tree, which, as it went to the Ground, did uptear severall small Plants by the Roots, methoughte such woulde be the Fall of dear *Father*, herein more sad than that of the Abbot of *Sion* and the *Charterhouse* Monks, inasmuch as, being celibate, they involve noe others in theire Ruin. Brave, holie Martyrs! how cheerfully they went to theire Death. I'm glad to have seene how pious Men may turn e'en an ignominious Sentence into a kind of Euthanasy. Dear *Father* bade me note how they bore themselves as Bridegrooms going to theire Marriage, and converted what mighte have beene a Shock to my surcharged Spiritts, into a Lesson of deepe and high Comfort.

One Thing hath grieved me sorelie. He mistooke Somewhat I sayd at parting for an Implication of my Wish that he shoulde yield up his Conscience. Oh no, dearest *Father*, that be far from me! It seems to have cut him to the Heart, for he hath writ that "none of the terrible Things that may befall him touch him soe nearlie as that his dearly beloved Child, whose Opinion he soe much values, shoulde desire him to overrule his Conscience." That be far from me, *Father*! I have writ to explayn the Matter, but his Reproach, undeserved though it be, hath troubled my Heart.

November.

Parliament will meet to-morrow. 'Tis expected *Father* and the good Bishop of *Rochester* will be attainted for Misprision of Treason by the slavish Members thereof; and though not given hithertoe unto much Heede of Omens and Bodements while our Hearts were light and our Courage high, yet now the coming Evill seemeth foreshadowed unto alle by I know not how many melancholick Presages, sent, for aught we know, in Mercy. Now that the days are dark and short, and the Nights stormy, we shun to linger much after Dusk in lone Chambers and Passages, and what was sayd of the Enemies of *Israel* may be nigh sayd of us, "that a falling Leaf shall chase them." I'm sure "a going in the Tops of the Mulberry Trees" on a blusterous Evening, is enow to draw us alle, Men, Mothers, and Maids, together in an Heap.... We goe aboute the House in Twos and Threes, and care not much to leave the Fireside. Last *Sunday* we had closed about the Hearth, and little *Bill* was a reading by the Fire-light how *Herodias'* Daughter danced off the Head of St. *John* the *Baptist*, when down comes an emptie Swallow's Nest tumbling adown the Chimnie, bringing with it enow of Soot, Smoke, and Rubbish to half smother us alle; but the Dust was nothing to the Dismay thereby occasioned, and I noted one or two of our bravest turn as pale as Death. Then, the Rats have skirmished and gallopped behind the Wainscoat more like a Troop of Horse than a Herd of such small Deer, to the infinite Annoyance of *Mother*, who coulde not be more firmly persuaded they were about to leave a falling House, if, like the scared Priests in the Temple of *Jerusalem*, she had heard a Voyce utter, "Let us depart hence." The round upper Half of the Cob-loaf rolled off the Table this Morning; and *Rupert*, as he picked it up, gave a Kind of Shudder, and muttered somewhat about a Head rolling from the Scaffold. Worse than this was o' *Tuesday* Night.... 'Twas Bed-time, and yet none were liking to goe, when, o' suddain, we hearde a Screech that made every Body's Heart thrill, followed by one or two hollow Groans. *Will* snatches up the Lamp and runs forth, I close following, and alle the others at our Heels; and after looking into sundrie deserted Cup-boards and Corners, we descend the broad Stone Steps of the Cellars, half way down which *Will*, stumbling over something he sees not, takes a flying Leap to clear himself down to the Bottom, luckily without extinguishing the Lamp. We find *Gillian* on the Steps in a Swoon; on bringing her to, she exclayms about a Ghost without a Head, wrapped in a Winding-sheet, that confronted her and then sank to the Ground as she entered the Vaults. We cast a fearfulle Look about, and descry a tall white Sack of Flour, recently overturned by the Rats, which clears up the Mystery, and procures *Gillian* a little Jeering; but we alle return to the Hall with fluttered Spiritts. Another Time I, going up to the Nurserie in the Dark, on hearing Baby cry, am passed on the Stairs by I know not what, breathing heavilie. I reache forthe my Arm, but pass cleare through the spirituall Nature, whatever it is, yet distinctlie feel my Cheek and Neck fanned by its Breath. I turn very faint, and get Nurse to goe with me when I return, bearing a Light, yet think it as well to say nought to distress the rest.

GILLIAN AND THE FLOUR SACKS.
Drawn by John Jellicoe

But worst of alle was last Night.... After I had beene in Bed awhile, I minded me that deare *Will* had not returned me *Father's* Letter. I awoke him, and asked if he had broughte it up Stairs; he sleepily replied he had not, soe I hastily arose, threw on a Cloke, took a Light, and entered the Gallery; when, half-way along it, between me and the pale Moonshine, I was scared to behold a slender Figure alle in white, with naked Feet and Arms extended. I stoode agaze, speechlesse, and to my Terror made out the Features of *Bess* ... her Eyes open, but vacant; then saw *John Dancey* softly stealing after her, and signing to me with his Finger on his Lips. She passed without noting me, on to *Father's* Door, there knelt as if in Prayer, making a low sort of Wail, while *Dancey*, with Tears running down his Cheeks, whispered, "'Tis the third Time of her thus sleep-walking ... the Token of how troubled a Mind!"

We disturbed her not, dreading that a suddain Waking might bring on Madness; soe after making Moan awhile, she kisses the senseless Door, rises up, moves towards her own Chamber, followed by *Dancey* and me, wrings her Hands a little, then lies down and graduallie falls into what seems a dreamlesse Sleep, we watching her in Silence till she's quiet, and then squeezing each other's Hands cre we part.

----*Will* was wide awake when I got back; he sayd, "Why, *Meg*, how long you have beene! coulde you not lighte on the Letter?" ... When I tolde him what had hindered me by the Way, he turned his Face to the Wall and wept.

Midnight.

The wild Wind is abroad, and, methinketh, *nothing else*. Sure, how it rages through our empty Courts! In such a Season, Men, Beasts, and Fowls cower beneath the Shelter of their rocking Walls, yet almost fear to trust them. Lord, I know that thou canst give the Tempest double Force, but do not, I beseech thee! Oh! have Mercy on the frail Dwelling and the Ship at Sea.

Dear little *Bill* hath ta'en a feverish Attack. I watch beside him whilst his Nurse sleeps. Earlie in the Night his Mind wandered, and he told me of a pretty pyebald Poney, noe bigger than a Bee, that had golden Housings and Barley-sugar Eyes; then dozed, but ever and anon kept starting up, crying, "Mammy dear!" and soft-lie murmured, "Oh!" when he saw I was by. At length I gave him my Forefinger to hold, which kept him ware of my Presence without speaking; but presentlie he stares hard towards the Foot of the Bed, and says fearfullie, "*Mother*, why hangs yon Hatchet in the Air, with its sharp Edge turned towards us?" I rise, move the Lamp, and say, "Do you see it now?" He sayth, "No, not now," and closes his Eyes. After a good Space, during the which I hoped he slept, he says in quite an altered Tone, most like unto soft, sweet Music, "There's a pretty little Cherub there now, alle Head and noe Body, with two little Wings aneath his Chin; but, for alle he's soe pretty, he is just like dear *Gaffer*, and seems to know me ... and he'll have a Body agayn too, I believe, by and by.... *Mother, Mother,* tell *Hobbinol* there's such a gentle Lamb in Heaven!" And soe, slept.

17th.

He's gone, my pretty...! slipt through my Fingers like a Bird! upfled to his own native Skies; and yet, whenas I think on him, I cannot choose but weepe.... Such a guilelesse little Lamb!... My Billy-bird! his Mother's owne Heart! — They are alle wondrous kind to me....

27th.

How strange that a little Child shoulde be permitted to suffer soe much Payn, when of such is the Kingdom of Heaven! But 'tis onlie transient, whereas a Mother makes it permanent, by thinking it over and over agayn. One Lesson it taughte us betimes, that a naturall Death is not, necessarilie, the most easie. We must alle die.... As poor *Patteson* was used to say, "The greatest King that ever was made, must bed at last with Shovel and Spade," ... and I'd sooner have my *Billy's* Baby Deathbed than King *Harry's*, or *Nan Boleyn's* either, however manie Years they may yet carry Matters with a high Hand. Oh, you Ministers of Evill, whoever ye be, visible or invisible, you shall not build a Wall between my God and me.... I've Something within me grows stronger and stronger, as Times grow more and more Evill; some woulde call it Resolution, but methinketh 'tis Faith.

Meantime, *Father's* Foes ... alack that anie can shew 'emselves such! are aiming, by fayr Seemings of friendlie Conference, to draw from him Admissions they can come at after noe other Fashion. The new *Solicitor Generall* hath gone to the Tower to deprive him of the few Books I have taken him from Time to Time.... Ah, Master *Rich*, you must deprive him of his Brains afore you can rob him of their Contents!... and, while having 'em packt up, he falls into easie Dialogue with him, as thus, ... "Why now, sure, Mr. *More*, were there an Act of Parliament made that all the Realm shoulde take me for King, you woulde take me for such with the Rest."

"Aye, that would I, Sir," returns *Father*.

"Forsooth, then," pursues *Rich*, "we'll suppose another Act that should make me the Pope. Woulde you not take me for Pope?"

"Or suppose another Case, Mr. *Rich*," returns *Father*, "that another Act shoulde pass, that GOD shoulde not be GOD, would you say well and good?"

"No, truly," returns the other hastily, "for no Parliament coulde make such Act lawful."

"True, as you say," repeats *Father*, "they coulde not," ... soe eluded the Net of the Fowler; but how miserable and unhandsome a Device to lay wait for him thus!

... I stole forthe, ere 'twas Lighte, this damp chill Morning, to pray beside the little Grave, but found dear *Daisy* there before me. How Christians love one another!

Will's Loss is as heavie as mine, yet he bears with me tenderlie. Yesternighte, he sayth to me half reproachfullie, "Am not I better unto thee than ten Sons?"

March, 1535.

Spring comes, that brings Rejuvenescence to the Land, and Joy to the Heart, but it brings none to us, for where Hope dieth, Joy dieth. But Patience, Soul; GOD's yet in the Aumry!

May 7.

Father arraigned.

July 1.

By Reason of *Will's* minding to be present at the Triall, which, for the Concourse of Spectators, demanded his earlie Attendance, he committed the Care of me, with *Bess*, to *Dancey*, who got us Places to see *Father* on his Way from the *Tower* to *Westminster Hall*. We coulde not come at him for the Crowd, but clambered on a Bench to gaze our very Hearts away after him as he went by, sallow, thin, greyhaired, yet in Mien not a Whit cast down. Wrapt in a coarse woollen Gown, and leaning on a Staff; which unwonted Support when *Bess* markt, she hid her Eyes on my Shoulder and wept sore, but soon lookt up agayn, though her Eyes were soe blinded, I think she coulde not see him. His Face was calm, but grave, as he came up, but just as he passed he caughte the Eye of some one in the Crowd, and smiled in his old, frank Way; then glanced up towards the Windows with the bright Look he hath soe oft cast to me at my Casement, but saw us not. I coulde not help crying "*Father*," but he heard me not; perchance 'twas soe best.... I woulde not have had his Face cloud at the Sighte of poor *Bessy's* Tears.

... *Will* tells me the Indictment was the longest ever hearde; on four Counts. First, his Opinion on the King's Marriage. Second, his writing sundrie Letters to the *Bishop of Rochester*, counselling him to hold out. Third, refusing to acknowledge his Grace's Supremacy. Fourth, his positive Deniall of it, and thereby willing to deprive the King of his Dignity and Title.

When the reading of this was over, the *Lord Chancellor* sayth, "Ye see how grievouslie you have offended the King his Grace, but and yet he is soe mercifulle, as that if ye will lay aside your Obstinacie, and change your Opinion, we hope ye may yet obtayn Pardon."

Father makes Answer ... and at Sounde of his deare Voyce alle Men hold their Breaths; ... "Most noble Lords, I have great Cause to thank your Honours for this your Courtesie ... but I pray ALMIGHTY GOD I may continue in the Mind I'm in, through his Grace, until Death."

They coulde not make goode their Accusation agaynst him. 'Twas onlie on the Last Count he could be made out a Traitor, and Proof of't had they none; how coulde they have? He shoulde have beene acquitted out of hand, 'steade of which, his bitter Enemy my *Lord Chancellor* called on him for his Defence. *Will* sayth there was a generall Murmur or Sigh ran through the Court. *Father*, however, answered the Bidding by beginning to expresse his Hope that the Effect of long Imprisonment mighte not have beene such upon his Mind and Body, as to impair his Power of rightlie meeting alle the Charges agaynst him ... when, turning faint with long standing, he staggered and loosed Hold of his Staff, whereon he was accorded a Seat. 'Twas but a Moment's Weakness of the Body, and he then proceeded frankly to avow his having always opposed the *King's* Marriage to his Grace himself, which he was soe far from thinking High Treason, that he shoulde rather have deemed it Treachery to have withholden his Opinion from his Sovereign King when solicited by him for his Counsell. His Letters to the good *Bishop* he proved to have been harmlesse. Touching his declining to give his Opinion, when askt, concerning the Supremacy, he alleged there coulde be noe Transgression in holding his Peace thereon, GOD only being cognizant of our Thoughts.

"Nay," interposeth the *Attorney Generall*, "your Silence was the Token of a malicious Mind."

"I had always understoode," answers *Father*, "that Silence stoode for Consent. *Qui tacet, consentire videtur;*" which made Sundrie smile. On the last Charge, he protested he had never spoken Word against the Law unto anie Man.

The Jury are about to acquit him, when up starts the *Solicitor Generall*, offers himself as Witness for the Crown, is sworn, and gives Evidence of his Dialogue with *Father* in the Tower, falselie adding, like a Liar as he is, that on his saying "No Parliament coulde make a Law that GOD shoulde not be GOD," *Father* had rejoyned, "No more coulde they make the King supreme Head of the Church."

I marvell the Ground opened not at his Feet. *Father* brisklie made Answer, "If I were a Man, my Lords, who regarded not an Oath, ye know well I needed not stand now at this Bar. And if the Oath which you, Mr. *Rich*, have just taken, be true, then I pray I may never see GOD in the Face. In good Truth, Mr. *Rich*, I am more sorry for your Perjurie than my Perill. You and I once dwelt long together in one Parish; your manner of Life and Conversation from your Youth up were familiar to me, and it paineth me to tell ye were ever held very light of your Tongue, a great Dicer and Gamester, and not of anie commendable Fame either there or in the *Temple*, the Inn to which ye have belonged. Is it credible, therefore, to your Lordships, that the Secrets of my Conscience touching the Oath, which I never woulde reveal, after the Statute once made, either to the King's Grace himself, nor to anie of you, my honourable Lords, I should have thus lightly blurted out in private Parley with Mr. *Rich*?"

In short, the Villain made not goode his Poynt: ne'erthelesse, the Issue of this black Day was aforehand fixed; my Lord *Audley* was primed with a virulent and venomous Speech; the Jury retired, and presentlie returned with a Verdict of Guilty; for they knew what the King's Grace woulde have 'em doe in that Case.

Up starts my Lord *Audley*;—commences pronouncing Judgment, when—

"My Lord," says *Father*, "in my Time, the Custom in these Cases was ever to ask the Prisoner before Sentence, whether he coulde give anie Reason why Judgment shoulde not proceed agaynst him."

My Lord, in some Confusion, puts the Question.

And then came the frightful Sentence.

Yes, yes, my Soul, I know; there were Saints of old sawn asunder. Men of whom the World was not worthy.

... Then he spake unto 'em his Mind; and bade his Judges and Accusers farewell; hoping that like as St. *Paul* was present and consenting unto St. *Stephen's* Death, and yet both were now holy Saints in Heaven, so he and they might speedilie meet there, joint Heirs of e'erlasting Salvation.

Meantime, poor *Bess* and *Cecilie*, spent with Grief and long waiting, were forct to be carried Home by *Heron*, or ever *Father* returned to his Prison. Was't less Feeling, or more Strength of Body, enabled me to bide at the Tower Wharf with *Dancey*? GOD knoweth. They brought him back by Water; my poor Sisters must have passed him.... The first Thing I saw was the Axe, *turned with its Edge towards him*— my first Note of his Sentence. I forct my Way through the Crowd ... some one laid a cold Hand on mine Arm; 'twas poor *Patteson*, soe changed I scarce knew him, with a Rosary of Gooseberries he kept running through his Fingers. He sayth, "Bide your Time, Mistress *Meg*; when he comes past, I'll make a Passage for ye; ... Oh, Brother, Brother! what ailed thee to refuse the Oath? *I've* taken it!" In another Moment, "Now, Mistress, now!" and flinging his Arms right and left, made a Breach through which I darted, fearlesse of Bills and Halberds, and did cast mine Arms about *Father's* Neck. He cries, "My *Meg*!" and hugs me to him as though our very Souls shoulde grow together. He sayth, "Bless thee, bless thee! Enough, enough, my Child; what mean ye, to weep and break mine Heart? Remember, though I die innocent, 'tis not without the Will of GOD, who coulde have turned mine Enemies' Hearts, if 'twere best; therefore possess your Soul in Patience. Kiss them alle for me, thus and thus ..." soe gave me back into *Dancey's* Arms, the Guards about him alle weeping; but I coulde not thus lose Sight of him for ever; soe, after a Minute's Pause, did make a second Rush, brake away from *Dancey*, clave to *Father* agayn, and agayn they had Pitie on me, and made Pause while I hung upon his Neck. This Time there were large Drops standing on his dear Brow; and the big Tears were swelling into his Eyes. He whispered, "*Meg*, for *Christ's* Sake don't unman me; thou'lt not deny my last Request?" I sayd, "Oh! no;" and at once loosened mine Arms. "God's Blessing be with you," he sayth with a last Kiss. I coulde not help crying, "My *Father*, my *Father!*" "The Chariot of *Israel*, and the Horsemen thereof!" he vehementlie whispers, pointing upwards with soe passionate a Regard, that I look up, almost expecting a beatific Vision; and when I turn about agayn, he's gone, and I have noe more Sense nor Life till I find myself agayn in mine owne Chamber, my Sisters chafing my Hands.

MORE RETURNING FROM HIS TRIAL.
Drawn by John Jellicoe

July 5th.

Alle's over now ... they've done theire worst, and yet I live. There were Women coulde stande aneath the Cross. The *Maccabees'* Mother— ... yes, my Soul, yes; I know—Nought but unpardoned Sin.... The Chariot of *Israel*.

6th.

Dr. *Clement* hath beene with us. Sayth he went up as blythe as a Bridegroom to be clothed upon with Immortality.

Rupert stoode it alle out. Perfect Love casteth out Feare. Soe did his.

17th.

My most precious Treasure is this deare Billet, writ with a Coal; the last Thing he sett his Hand to, wherein he sayth, "I never liked your Manner towards me better than when you kissed me last."

19th.

They have let us bury his poor mangled Trunk; but, as sure as there's a Sun in Heaven, I'll have his Head!—before another Sun hath risen, too. If wise Men won't speed me, I'll e'en content me with a Fool.

I doe think Men, for the most Part, be Cowards in theire Hearts ... moral Cowards. Here and there, we find one like *Father*, and like *Socrates*, and like ... this and that one, I mind not theire Names just now; but in the Main, methinketh they lack the moral Courage of Women. Maybe, I'm unjust to 'em just now, being crost.

July 20th.

I lay down, but my Heart was waking. Soon after the first Cock crew, I hearde a Pebble cast agaynst my Lattice, knew the Signall, rose, dressed, stole softlie down and let myself out. I knew the Touch of the poor Fool's Fingers; his Teeth were chattering, 'twixt Cold and Fear, yet he laught aneath his Breath as he caught my Arm and dragged me after him, whispering, "Fool and fayr Lady will cheat 'em yet." At the Stairs lay a Wherry with a Couple of Boatmen, and one of 'em stepping up to me, cries, "Alas for ruth, Mistress *Meg*, what is't ye do? Art mad to go on this Errand?" I sayd, "I shall be mad if I goe not, and succeed too—put me in, and push off."

We went down the River quietlie enow—at length reach *London Bridge* Stairs. *Patteson*, starting up, says, "Bide ye all as ye are," and springs aland and runneth up to the Bridge. Anon, returns, and sayth, "Now, Mistress, alle's readie ... readier than ye wist ... come up quickly, for the Coast's clear." *Hobson* (for 'twas he) helps me forth, saying, "God speed ye, Mistress.... An' I dared, I woulde goe with ye." ... Thought I, there be others in that Case.

Nor lookt I up till aneath the Bridge-gate, when casting upward a fearsome Look, I beheld the dark Outline of the ghastly yet precious Relic; and, falling into a Tremour, did wring my Hands and exclaym, "Alas, alas, that Head hath lain full manie a Time in my Lap, woulde God, woulde God it lay there now!" When, o' suddain, I saw the Pole tremble and sway towards me; and stretching forth my Apron, I did in an Extasy of Gladness, Pity, and Horror, catch its Burthen as it fell. *Patteson*, shuddering, yet grinning, cries under his Breath, "Managed I not well, Mistress? Let's speed away with our Theft, for Fools and their Treasures are soon parted; but I think not they'll follow hard after us, neither, for there are Well-wishers to us on the Bridge. I'll put ye into the Boat and then say, God speed ye, Lady, with your Burthen."

"NOR LOOKT I UP TILL ANEATH THE BRIDGE-GATE."
Drawn by Herbert Railton

July 23rd.

Rizpah, Daughter of *Aiah*, did watch her Dead from the Beginning of Harvest until the latter Rain, and suffered neither the Birds of the Air to light on them by Day, nor the wild Beasts of the Field by Night. And it was told the King, but he intermeddled not with her.

Argia stole *Polynices'* Body by Night and buried it, for the which, she with her Life did willingly pay Forfeit. *Antigone*, for aiding in the pious Theft, was adjudged to be buried alive. *Artemisia* did make herself her loved one's Shrine, by drinking his Ashes. Such is the Love of Women; many Waters cannot quench it, neither can the Floods drown it. I've hearde *Bonvisi* tell of a poor *Italian* Girl, whose Brothers did slay her Lover; and in Spite of them she got his Heart, and buried it in a Pot of Basil, which she watered Day and Night with her Tears, just as I do my Coffer. *Will* has promised it shall be buried with me; layd upon my Heart; and since then, I've beene easier.

He thinks he shall write *Father's* Life, when he gets more composed, and we are settled in a new Home. We are to be cleared out o' this in alle Haste; the King grutches at our lingering over *Father's* Footsteps, and gazing on the dear familiar Scenes associate with his Image; and yet, when the News of the bloody Deed was taken to him, as he sate playing at Tables with Queen *Anne*, he started up and scowled at her, saying, "Thou art the Cause of this Man's Death!" *Father* might well say, during our last precious Meeting in the Tower, "'Tis I, *Meg*, not the King, that love Women. They belie him; he onlie loves himself." Adding, with his own sweet Smile, "Your *Gaffer* used to say that Women were a Bag of Snakes, and that the Man who put his Hand therein woulde be lucky if he founde one Eel among them alle; but 'twas onlie in Sport, *Meg*, and he owned that I had enough Eels to my Share to make a goodly Pic, and called my House the Eel-pie House to the Day of his Death. 'Twas our Lord *Jesus* raised up Women, and shewed Kindnesse unto 'em; and they've kept theire Level, in the Main, ever since."

I wish *Will* may sett down everie Thing of *Father's* saying he can remember; how precious will his Book then be to us! But I fear me, these Matters adhere not to a Man's Memory ... he'll be telling of his Doings as Speaker and Chancellor, and his saying this and that in Parliament. Those are the Matters Men like to write and to read; he won't write it after my Fashion.

I had a Misgiving of *Will's* Wrath, that Night, 'speciallie if I failed; but he called me his brave *Judith*. Indeed I was a Woman bearing a Head, but one that had oft lain on my Shoulder.

My Thoughts beginne to have Connexion now; but till last Night, I slept not. 'Twas scarce Sunsett. *Mercy* had been praying beside me, and I lay outside my Bed, inclining rather to Stupor than Sleep. O' suddain, I have an Impression that some one is leaning over me, though I hear 'em not, nor feel theire Breath. I start up, cry "*Mercy!*" but she's not there, nor anie one else. I turn on my Side and become heavie to Sleep; but or ere I drop quite off, agayn I'm sensible or apprehensive of some living Consciousness between my closed Eyelids and the setting Sunlight; agayn start up and stare about, but there's Nothing. Then I feel like ... like *Eli*, maybe, when the Child *Samuel* came to him twice; and Tears well into mine Eyes, and I close 'em agayn, and say in mine Heart, "If he's at Hand, oh, let me see him next Time ... the third Time's lucky." But 'steade of this, I fall into quiet, balmy, dreamlesse Sleep. Since then, I've had an abiding, assuring Sense of Help, of a Hand upholding me, and smoothing and glibbing the Way before me.

We must yield to the Powers that be. At this Present, we are weak, but they are strong; they are honourable, but we are despised. They have made us a Spectacle unto the World, and, I think, Europe will ring with it; but at this present Hour, they will have us forth of our Home, though we have as yet no certayn Dwelling-Place, and must flee as scared Pigeons from their Dove-cot. No Matter; our

Men are willing to labour, and our Women to endure: being reviled, we bless; being persecuted, we suffer it. Onlie I marvell how anie honest Man, coming after us, will be able to eat a Mouthful of Bread with a Relish within these Walls. And, methinketh, a dishonest Man will have sundrie Frights from the *Lares* and *Lemures.* There'll be Dearth o' black Beans in the Market.

Flow on, bright shining *Thames.* A good brave Man hath walked aforetime on your Margent, himself as bright, and usefull, and delightsome as be you, sweet River. And like you, he never murmured; like you, he upbore the weary, and gave Drink to the Thirsty, and reflected Heaven in his Face. I'll not swell your full Current with any more fruitless Tears. There's a River, whose Streams make glad the City of our GOD. He now rests beside it. Good Christian Folks, as they hereafter pass this Spot, upborne on thy gentle Tide, will, maybe, point this Way, and say—"There dwelt Sir *Thomas More;*" but whether they doe or not, *Vox Populi* is a very inconsiderable Matter. Who would live on theire Breath? They hailed St. *Paul* as *Mercury,* and then stoned him, and cast him out of the City, supposing him to be dead. Theire Favourite of to-day may, for what they care, goe hang himself to-morrow in his Surcingle. Thus it must be while the World lasts; and the very Racks and Scrues wherewith they aim to overcome the nobler Spiritt, onlie test and reveal its Power of Exaltation above the heaviest Gloom of Circumstance.

Interfecistis, interfecistis Hominem omnium Anglorum optimum.

FINIS

Lector House believes that a society develops through a two-fold approach of continuous learning and adaptation, which is derived from the study of classic literary works spread across the historic timeline of literature records. Therefore, we aim at reviving, repairing and redeveloping all those inaccessible or damaged but historically as well as culturally important literature across subjects so that the future generations may have an opportunity to study and learn from past works to embark upon a journey of creating a better future.

This book is a result of an effort made by Lector House towards making a contribution to the preservation and repair of original ancient works which might hold historical significance to the approach of continuous learning across subjects.

HAPPY READING & LEARNING!

LECTOR HOUSE LLP
E-MAIL: lectorpublishing@gmail.com

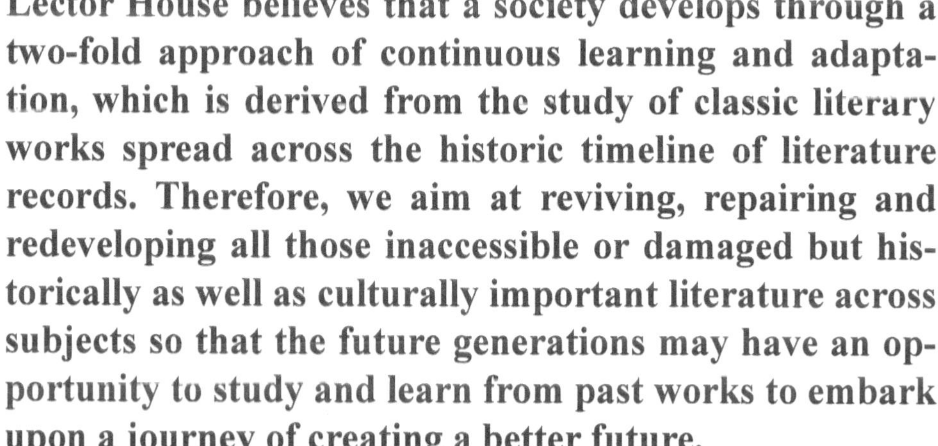

9 789353 449087